THE
BUTTERFLY RECLUSE

THERESE HECKENKAMP

ɪ𝑻ᴘ

Ivory Tower Press

www.ivorytowerpress.com

© 2019 by Therese Heckenkamp

www.thereseheckenkamp.com

All rights reserved.

ISBN 978-0-9968057-2-8

This is a work of fiction. All the characters, organizations, places, and events portrayed in this novel are either products of the author's imagination or are used fictitiously. Any resemblance to actual persons, living or dead, is entirely coincidental.

Scripture verses taken from the Douay-Rheims Holy Bible.

No part of this book may be reproduced, stored in a retrieval system or transmitted in any form or by any means without the prior written permission of the publisher, except by a reviewer who may quote brief passages in a review.

Cover design by BetiBup33 Studio Design

Published by
Ivory Tower Press
www.ivorytowerpress.com

Also by Therese Heckenkamp:

After the Thaw
Frozen Footprints
Past Suspicion

*For my daughters,
as well as anyone who has ever appreciated
the delicate beauty of a butterfly.*

*"Who will give me wings . . .
and I will fly and be at rest?"*

— Psalm 54:7

Chapter 1

I think the butterflies knew what was coming that day—that *he* was coming, and that life as we knew it was about to change.

They didn't let on, of course. They simply continued their usual activity, flitting and floating, luring me outside.

One particularly large monarch caught my eye as it alighted on a marigold a mere two steps in front of me.

I froze, not even allowing myself the motion of a smile. The delicate orange-and-black wings, designed with more intricacy than any human could accomplish, fanned rhythmically, almost thoughtfully, while flashing their bitter toxicity to any birds that might otherwise target them as a tasty fast-food meal.

Barely breathing, I eased forward in excruciating slow motion. The monarch's antennae bobbed, smelling the sweet nectar as its straw-like black tongue uncurled and prodded deep inside the flower.

The butterfly sipped, tongue pumping like a slender

hose. I enjoyed the sight for a moment before raising my Nikon to frame the picture in my viewfinder, to capture this fleeting moment in all its peaceful, fragile splendor before—

VRRROOOMM!

The intrusive motor roar jolted my shoulders. I dropped my camera and it bounced on its strap against my chest.

The butterfly took off.

VRRROOOMM!

The ear-shattering noise increased, and sound waves shook the air. I cringed. Something—*someone*—was coming up my driveway. A rare occurrence, and one I'd rather not deal with.

Since I couldn't disappear like the butterfly, I darted through the flowers to the side of my house, slipping from sight just as a motorcycle roared into view.

A motorcycle, on my property.

The thought turned my stomach.

The rider must be lost or have the wrong house. He'd leave soon enough once he rang my doorbell and no one answered. I followed the horizontal vinyl siding of my house until I rounded the corner to my backyard.

My haven.

No motorcycle here.

The marigolds, so bright they radiated yellow and orange, called to the butterflies. *Come, taste, stay a while . . .*

Royal purple and passionate pink flowers adorned dozens of milkweed plants. Red and yellow zinnia blooms completed the garden. My peace slowly returning, I sighed and watched the visiting butterflies sample the nectar.

One monarch perched on the edge of an impressive flower cluster, hanging so that its wings blinked open and closed as if winking at the ground.

Thoughtfully, I traced the surface of my camera. My photo opportunity in the front garden had been cut short, but maybe this would be a better one, a creative viewpoint I'd never tried before.

I slipped to the ground and lay back against the grass. Blades tickling my neck, I scooched into position one centimeter at a time until I saw the orange-and-black wings pulsing and the butterfly bobbing on the flower above me.

Perfect.

Easing my camera into position, I framed the shot. I'd snapped many butterfly pictures in my twenty-three years, but never one like this. Heart singing with satisfaction, I poised my finger for the right moment—full wingspan—to take the shot. No way would I lose this one.

"Hello?" A man's voice punctured the silence. Footsteps cracked branches and crushed plants as the guy approached with no regard for my garden, butterflies, or photo op.

Milkweed leaves quivered above me, but I didn't move. Amazingly, neither did the butterfly.

"Hello? Anyone here?" The voice rose louder, closer, twinging my nerves. I clutched my camera protectively.

Stems rustled beside me, followed by a pause that

made me hold my breath.

A terrible weight smashed onto my shin, a bolt of pain zinged up my leg, and my breath escaped in a shriek. I popped to a sitting position, and the butterfly darted away, along with my hopes of the perfect picture.

The man stumbled backward, looking appropriately shocked. I reached for my lower leg, half expecting to see a boot imprint, and rubbed the sore spot. Words scrambled through my head, but my lips stayed sealed.

They were so used to silence.

"I'm so sorry—I can't believe I stepped on you. Man, that sounds terrible." Looking chagrined, the stranger shook his head. "It *is* terrible. But I just didn't see you there." He edged closer. "Are you okay?" He dropped to one knee beside me. So close. Warm air stirred around us, unsettling, as if charged with electricity.

I edged away, then pushed myself up off the ground. "I-I'm fine." Just a little flustered.

"Doesn't sound like you're fine." He stood, and I glimpsed his eyes, rich blue. Morpho butterfly blue. Intense and stunning. Concerned.

What to do? What to say? For no reason at all, I felt myself blushing. Already, I was surely making an odd impression, proving the town gossips right.

I tilted my face downward and spotted his feet, his big, heavy black boots. They had to feel sweltering on a hot summer day like today.

The man's gaze must have followed mine because he said, "You're not wearing any shoes."

My toes curled, gripping the earth. "I wasn't expecting any company."

"Aren't you worried you'll step on something sharp?"

"No, I'm careful. Going barefoot feels wonderful in the summer." I couldn't help glancing almost sympathetically at his boots. "You should try it sometime."

He laughed, the sound rich, almost soothing. I tried to join in, but didn't quite know how.

My nerves fluttered. Who was this man and what was he doing on my property?

He scratched his head. I was surprised he could find it through such thick blond hair. He glanced from me to the spot where I'd lain mere moments before. "So why were you hiding in the weeds?"

My eyes widened. "Weeds?" After all the work I'd done to cultivate them? I covered a tiny laugh. "Oh, no, these aren't weeds." My fingers brushed a leaf tenderly. "They're part of my garden, my butterfly garden. Monarchs love milkweed."

"Yeah? Weed's in the name, but they're not weeds. Sure . . . makes perfect sense." He smiled and tapped his temple. "Got it."

"And I wasn't hiding." I shifted my camera. "Well, I guess I was . . . From the butterflies, that is. I was only trying to take a picture."

He glanced at the ground, and his voice came out incredulous. "Of the dirt?"

"No, of a butterfly. From a unique perspective." My shoulders bounced a little shrug. "But you scared it away."

He nodded. "And then I stepped on you."

I shrugged again. "You didn't mean to. It was an accident."

He squinted at me. "I'm making a bad first impression, aren't I?"

"No . . . I, um, I'm just wondering why you're here, that's all."

"Okay, well here goes." He squared his shoulders. "I'm here to ask you a favor."

A favor? From me? Again, a laugh stirred in my throat, a reflex my body had almost forgotten.

"Hear me out. It's not really a favor so much as a business proposition."

Business? I blinked. Did I look like a business woman? Certainly not. He must have me confused with someone.

He stuck out his hand. "My name's Harvey."

Feeling awkward, I met his palm. The firmness of his grasp and hearty handshake startled me. When his eyes assessed me, I wondered what he noticed. My hesitant expression, my messy brown hair, my plain T-shirt? Hopefully not the grass stain on my knee. I angled myself to try to shield it.

"Like I said, I'm sorry I hurt you. I am, really." He released my hand and I glanced at it. My palm felt different somehow. Warmer, hypersensitive. How long had it been since I'd shaken someone's hand? Touched someone's hand, for that matter?

"Lila," I said, suddenly remembering I should have introduced myself. "I mean, that's my name."

He brightened. "Nice to meet you, Lila. I hope you don't mind, but I saw you head back here and just followed you. Don't worry, I'm not selling anything. I'm here to buy. And I'm willing to pay top dollar."

Confused, I glanced around. "But I don't have anything to sell."

"Sure you do." A grin split his face and creased the corners of his eyes. "I've heard all about you."

Oh dear, I wished he hadn't. I could just imagine . . .

"You raise butterflies, right? Lots of them. So many that people even call you the butterfly rec—" He cleared his throat. "Uh, girl. The butterfly girl, yeah. And I'm in need of butterflies, that's all. For a butterfly release, and I heard you're the one to talk to. Am I right?"

I took a moment to process his words. It was almost funny that he thought I didn't know people called me the butterfly recluse. How kind of him to want to shield me from the fact.

Even so, I shook my head. "I'm very sorry, but I can't help you. My butterflies aren't a business, and I would never sell them. Why, that would be like selling a . . . a rainbow. Or . . . a star."

His gaze intensified. "People do that, you know. Sell stars."

What? My jaw fell. "You're joking. No one owns the stars. They belong to God."

God. I really didn't want to think about Him, and how He controlled everything. Everyone. I clamped my mouth shut as my stomach twisted and my thoughts headed for a black hole.

Harvey's words pulled me back. "Well, technically people sell the right to name the stars. Kinda the same thing, though."

Sounded suspicious to me.

A swallowtail butterfly flew by, and my gaze wandered, following its irresistible course. Where was it headed? What would it see on its way?

"You sure like butterflies."

My cheeks warmed. "I do."

Harvey nodded. "So does Sally, so you must know how much a butterfly release would mean to her. I can't refuse the bride-to-be her most important wedding request. What'll make you say yes? There's gotta be something. Name your price."

"It's not about money. I just don't like it, the whole idea of it, and neither do they."

"They . . ." Turning his head, he glanced around. "They . . . who?"

"The butterflies."

He stared, forcing those blue eyes on me. "It's not like I'm asking to kill the things. Sheesh. We're letting them go, setting them free. Win-win. What could be better?"

"Maybe not locking them up in the first place? Some people who do butterfly releases even put individual live butterflies flat into envelopes. *Envelopes*—just so each guest can let one go." I watched his reaction carefully.

He made a face. "I'm not gonna do that."

"Good, because some of them wouldn't make it. Imagine the wedding statement that would make: 'Best wishes for a long and happy marriage, and oh, by the way, here's your dead butterfly.'" I made a motion as if shaking something free from an envelope, then pointed to the ground. "'Try not to step on it.'"

He started to laugh, then snorted it short.

My mouth wasn't sure whether to smile or frown. He seemed like a nice enough guy. Not that I knew any men to judge him by. Old-time actors on classic TV probably didn't count.

But I supposed it was time I sent him on his way. He was a stranger, after all, and I did live alone on an isolated stretch of land. "I'm sorry I can't help you, but I'm sure you'll find someone who will."

"I won't. There's no one else local, and there's not enough time. The wedding's in less than a month." Harvey spread his hands. "I'm out of options. You're my last hope."

Such exaggeration. Such determination. "Sorry, but maybe it's time to think about a dove release." I paused. "Don't put those in envelopes, either."

I headed for my sliding back door, hoping that today it wouldn't stick as it so often did. I grasped the handle. "Goodbye."

"Just think about it, will you? Tell me you'll at least do that."

"No, I'm sorry, but my answer's not going to change." No point in wasting more of his time or giving him false hope. I swallowed a grunt as I tugged at my door. Of all the days to stick—

"Here, let me help you with that—"

"No!"

But he'd already pulled the door from me, yanking it open wide—so much wider than the crack I typically slipped through.

A cloud of orange-and-black wings fluttered out the door and past our faces, rising and dispersing in all directions to the sky.

I took in the beautiful sight—the weightlessness, the grace, the freedom—with a wistful smile. "There goes your butterfly release."

Chapter 2

Harvey turned wide eyes to me, his face flushing, reflecting guilt. "That wasn't supposed to happen, was it?"

I opened my mouth to explain, but he turned and took off after the monarchs. "Don't worry, I'll get them." He glanced over his shoulder. "You got a net?"

My lips suppressed a smile. "Yes, but—"

"Get it!" He raced around my yard like a madman, arms and hands snatching at nothing. For the sake of the delicate butterfly wings, I was glad he didn't stand a chance of snagging anything but air.

I lifted my camera, aimed, and captured the bizarre sight with a dozen rapid-fire shots before stepping into my sunroom and closing the door.

I clicked the lock into place.

Careful of the several remaining butterflies, as well as rows of shiny green chrysalises and numerous potted milkweed plants dotted with caterpillars, I drew the drapes against the sunlight.

"Sorry, my friends. Just till he leaves."

I slipped through the house, closing every shade, my heart pumping fast, sending a belated blend of excitement and confusion through my veins. I couldn't decipher which emotion outweighed the other. Both were disconcerting.

What had just happened? One-on-one human interaction was scarce in my world. It had been so long since I'd spoken more than a few words to anyone.

I wasn't sure how I felt about it.

Abrupt banging on the back door jolted me. "Hello?" Harvey called. "Where'd you go? Are you there?" A pause, then another knock. I imagined him scratching his head, wondering if he'd imagined the entire odd encounter. "This mean you're not getting the net?"

He raised his voice much louder than necessary. "Look, I'm sorry. I really am. But you've gotta know I didn't mean to let them out."

He thought I was angry? Oh dear, I hadn't meant to imply that. I was just worn out from the conversation and had no more to say. I crouched in the dimness near a butterfly resting on a leaf. Slowly, I offered my fingertip to the butterfly's feet and willed it to climb aboard. *Trust me.*

"How was I supposed to know you had an entire house full of them?" His voice dropped a notch. "Is that even legal?"

My spine stiffened and I pursed my lips. *One room. Not the "entire house."* Though some of the butterflies might stray into other rooms on occasion, they preferred the bright warmth of the sunroom full of their favorite flowers, as well as the refreshing birdbath-turned-butterfly-bath.

"Hello?"

Goodness, he was making it difficult to retreat into myself.

The butterfly, which I fondly called Wingly, crept onto my finger, tiny black feet gripping with a barely perceptible touch that tickled and prickled like the hook side of Velcro. I moved Wingly nearer to me and whispered, "He's leaving, don't worry."

I stroked the air directly above the butterfly's wings, finding comfort in the motion. I lingered at the shriveled hole that marred his upper-right wing. This poor little guy had emerged from his chrysalis with the flaw, and because of it, he'd never truly fly. He wouldn't last in the wild, so I'd care for him here as long as he needed. Wouldn't be long, a week or two . . . a few months at most.

I liked to think he felt safe when I held him, enjoyed when I gave him a ride on my finger, the air gliding past his wings in the only way it ever would.

The back door finally remained silent. I moved to the foyer and listened near the front door. Much as I hated the noise, I wanted to hear the motorcycle roar away so I could finally relax.

My doorbell trilled, startling me.

I stepped back, then paced, worried. Should I open it?

No, I'd said all I needed to. And what if Harvey tried to come inside? The mere thought overwhelmed me.

He seemed harmless enough, but one couldn't be too careful.

He knocked a few times. "Are you at least going to give me an answer about selling some butterflies?"

I lifted Wingly to eye level and whispered with a slight smile, "I do believe your brain is bigger than his." Wingly bobbed his thready black antennae in what I chose to think was agreement.

A few quiet seconds ticked by.

"Right." Harvey rapped the door with one quick staccato beat. "Okay then. No problem, you think on it and let me know."

I made a *pfft* noise through my lips, unintentionally releasing a puff of air onto Wingly. He fluttered his wings as if perturbed.

Sorry, buddy.

Silence finally met me. No more knocking, no more doorbell, no more loud man-voice. Good. Harvey must finally be leaving.

But I still hadn't heard the motorcycle. My ears prickled, waiting. What was taking so long?

I stepped to the edge of the closest window. Discreet as possible, I shifted a slat of blinds and peeked out in time to see him stroll to his shiny, obviously expensive motorcycle.

Even from a distance, I couldn't help noticing the strong tilt of his chin and the confidence in his step. He pulled a helmet over his messy crop of hair, then straddled his motorcycle. The bike looked as if it was made for him, as if money was no object.

Hopefully his Sally would appreciate the effort he'd

put into trying to line up a butterfly release for her, even if he hadn't succeeded. Not like a little thing like butterflies would make or break their wedding.

His posture radiated determination, and I was sure he'd figure something else out.

As he roared away, I had no regrets about turning him down.

And I was very relieved to see the motorcycle go.

～

After opening the drapes and returning daylight to the sunroom, I watered flowers, pinched off dead blooms, and discarded withered leaves.

I paced restlessly until dropping into my seat at the computer and proceeding to upload my latest batch of photos.

I cropped, retouched, and, most of all, returned again and again to the picture of Harvey in my backyard, because . . . well, there he was: a man. In my backyard. Surely my life couldn't get any stranger than that.

Tilting my head, I examined the photo from every angle. No matter how critical I tried to be, I couldn't deny that it was a good picture. Something about it was hilarious, yet endearing.

Harvey looked strong, yet gentle—not so much as if he was battling the butterflies as playing with them.

I decided not to post this image for sale with my others on the stock-photo website where I earned royalties. After all, I didn't have his permission—but even if I did, I didn't think I'd post it. It didn't really fit with my typical work.

My fingers fidgeted with the computer mouse, and I heard a ding as a message popped up on-screen.

Hey girl, wrote my friend Jess. *What's happening?*

I typed rapidly. *Just uploading some new pics.*

Yeah? Cool. So what're you waiting for? Send them my way!

I smiled. I'd met Jess, my overly enthusiastic friend, on a homeschool forum over five years ago, and we'd hit it off from the start.

And when my family was no longer there for me, she still was, even if only through Wi-Fi and a keyboard.

While I also kept in occasional touch with a few childhood friends who'd moved away, Jess, the friend I'd never even met in person, was the one I'd grown closest to.

With a few taps, I now sent her my entire batch of pictures, even the Harvey ones. For some reason, my stomach flipped at the realization.

Seconds plodded by, and though I wanted to grab a glass of water, I remained stuck to my seat, my gaze glued to the screen.

Jess's opinion was the only one that mattered.

Whoa, Lila. An eye-popping emoticon appeared. *Great work, as always, but—sound an alarm—there's a person in one of those pics! And not just any person—a guy! You holding out on me? What's that all about? Hurry up and answer. None of your long, thoughtful pauses while you think up the perfect response. Just type! Times like this I really wish I had your number. Hint, hint.*

Nice try. She could hint all she wanted, but she knew

I wouldn't give it. She knew I was comfortable with a set level of friendship, one that was relatively anonymous, with no pressure, controlled on my terms within the obscurity of cyberspace.

I detested phone calls. Ever since getting that one . . .

I shook the memory from my mind.

Jess understood.

One of these days we'd get around to meeting in person, I supposed, but we lived two states apart and just hadn't found the right time yet.

Sucking in a breath, I typed, *Just a guy trying to buy some of my butterflies. Can you believe that?*

Is he good-looking?

Trust her to ask that.

Hard to tell from the pics, she continued, *but I'm betting that's a big fat yes.*

I glanced up at the ticking clock above my computer. How to answer that?

Hello??? appeared on my screen. *Does your slowness give you away?*

Springing to action, I made my fingers fly over the keys. *Stop it! You'd probably think he's good-looking. Me, I don't see how that's relevant to anything.*

Oh yeah? I've known you over five years, and I still don't even get to visit.

He didn't get to, he just showed up uninvited, all pushy and loud and—

You're interested in him? And he's interested in you? Is he visiting again?

No, no, and NO! And for your information, he's getting married soon—which is why he wanted my butterflies. For a release, for his bride on their wedding day . . .

And I rambled on and on in an attempt to bore her into signing off. But she never lost interest in fishing for what she called "all the juicy details."

I finally told her I had to go because my butterflies were calling me.

Chapter 3

Late the next morning, I stood in my backyard hanging wet laundry on my clothesline when I heard Harvey's voice behind me.

"Hello again."

With my hands frozen on a lace undergarment, my head whipped around. "You!"

How unexpected. How—I turned back to my clothesline—embarrassing.

Damp underwear danced in the breeze—unmentionables that should also remain unseen by anyone but me.

My hands began yanking, almost ripping, clothes from the line in a frantic effort to make them vanish. What were the chances Harvey hadn't noticed them yet?

"Need any help?"

"No!" I pummeled the clothes into a hopefully indistinguishable mass in my basket. Wooden clothespins punctuated the clothesline above me like a row of miniature fenceposts.

"Okay." He scratched his neck. "It's just . . . you seem awful desperate to get your laundry down." He glanced at the blue sky. "Doesn't look like rain to me, so if you're worried about things getting wet—" He squinted. "But hey, they don't even look dry yet."

As in, he was *looking* at them? Oh, I was mortified.

"And weren't you actually hanging stuff up, not taking it down?"

"Forget the laundry." *Please.* "Why did you come back?" I stood in front of the basket and crossed my arms. "I told you yesterday that I'm not selling you any butterflies."

My mother would have been appalled at my lack of manners and hospitality, my father would have been proud of my boldness, and my little brother and sister would have been stunned.

Would have.

Would have.

I swallowed hard and pushed my lips together.

"I know, and I'm sorry if I caught you at a bad time." His gaze strayed to the laundry basket.

I used my foot to shove it behind a bush, relieved I didn't make things worse by dumping it over in the process. "How did you sneak up on me? Why didn't I hear your motorcycle?"

"I cut the engine early and walked up the drive, but I wasn't trying to sneak up. I was just afraid that if you heard me, you'd hide inside again and—"

"I wasn't *hiding*. I was—" I searched for the right word. The sun blazed on my skin, heating my entire body. "I was just—done. Tired of telling you no over and over. You really should take a hint."

"Noted. Or maybe"—hope sparked in Harvey's eyes—"you could tell me yes?"

Exasperated, I leveled a sharp gaze at him.

"Okay, okay. Taking the hint." He cleared his throat. "I really only came to tell you I'm sorry for yesterday." Hesitating, he brought his right hand into view. "And give you this."

He held a small flowering bush in a little black pot. "I know it doesn't make up for the butterflies I let out, but—"

"I don't keep butterflies prisoners, if that's what you think." My face flamed. I had to set him straight. "I raise them, to help increase and revive the butterfly population—especially the monarchs—but I release them when they're strong and their wings are ready. I would have released all those ones yesterday anyway."

The relief that came over his face was so genuine, my annoyance fizzled. "I do keep a few that can't fly properly or that wouldn't survive on their own, but I don't hoard butterflies like . . . like some people do cats. I don't like cats. They chase butterflies and play with them before they kill them." *Get to the point, Lila.* "I also don't sell butterflies." My words and reasoning began to feel fumbly in my mouth.

He still held the plant out like a peace offering, and I blinked at it.

"It's a butterfly bush," he said.

Yes, I recognized the tiny star-shaped pink flowers. It was beautiful, but . . . "You didn't have to do that."

He shrugged. "I know, but I thought it'd make a good addition to your garden. If you've got a shovel, I can plant it for you right now."

I twisted my fingers together and struggled for words. "You don't have to, really."

"Come on, I want to." He hefted the dirty roots from the thin plastic pot. "Besides, it needs a home. You don't want it to die, do you?" He gave me a "gotcha" grin.

"Fine, okay." A little thrill ran through me at the thought of keeping the bush.

"Great." He glanced around. "Where do you want it? And I'll still need a shovel."

"You mean you didn't haul one of those over here, too?" I pictured him riding his motorcycle one-handed, butterfly bush gripped in the other hand, wind tearing at the leaves and flowers. The bush should be bare by now.

"Nah. The plant fit in my saddlebag just fine, but I figured a gardener like you would have a shovel handy."

"Maybe. Then again . . . " I tapped a finger against my chin. "A gardener who specializes in growing *weeds* may not." It was my turn to flash a "gotcha" grin. I wasn't quite sure if I managed it, but I enjoyed trying.

He chuckled, and I headed to my shed to grab the tool, still feeling a bit blindsided by his appearance, the gift, and, most of all, the conversation.

I didn't have conversations. Not with people, and certainly not face-to-face, with spoken words. Why was I letting him linger?

It's for the butterflies, I reasoned as I fished a large

shovel from the shed. I glanced over my shoulder and saw him stride across the lawn as if assessing a spot for planting. My eyes narrowed. He'd better steer clear of my laundry basket.

I already had the perfect spot in mind, a location in full sun and in direct sight of my kitchen window.

He accepted the shovel. "Much as you like butterflies, I'm surprised you don't already have one of these bushes. You don't, do you?"

"No." It was on my list of things to buy in person, not online, but I rarely ventured out to shop in the real world.

"Okay, good. I wasn't sure, but either way I figured someone like you couldn't have too many."

Someone like me. I wondered what he meant by that. Someone who liked butterflies? Someone who liked to garden? Someone who was known for being a recluse?

I nodded, then watched him stab the shovel into the ground with a deep sluicing sound.

He heaved out several loads of earth before setting the bush in the hole. Then he broke up the packed dirt clumps and covered the roots, filling the hole back in, turning his hands filthy.

I pulled a hose up from the side of the house. "It looks very nice, and I'm sure the butterflies will love it. Thank you."

He propped the shovel in one grimy hand, then wiped sweat from his forehead with his bare arm. "You're welcome."

I aimed a steady stream of water at the base of the

bush. "But this doesn't mean I owe you." My voice came out soft, and I tried to make it strong. "Or that I'll reconsider selling you butterflies."

"Maybe not, or maybe it does. Something tells me you will." He gave me a smug grin. It felt like a taunt.

Without thinking, I reacted by turning the hose on him. Washed the grin right off.

"Hey!" He stumbled back in surprise at the cold blast. His hands shot forward to block the spray. "Okay, okay! I'm outta here!"

Something like disappointment twinged within me as he hurried away, following the snaking hose down the slope.

Funny or not, spraying him had been rather rude, especially after what he'd just done for me, even if he did have ulterior motives.

But it was a hot day, and he'd been covered with dirt. Truthfully, I'd done him a favor. In fact, I wouldn't mind—

The hose popped from my grasp, and I turned just in time to register that Harvey had yanked it away. Now he stood aiming the nozzle at me, his "gotcha" grin in place.

The cold stream hit me full force. I shrieked, sputtered on a mouthful of water, and ran, but the chilly droplets found me, quickly covering me in a wet glaze. He laughed, a deep, hearty sound. My ears drank it in.

Though shocked by his actions, I was more alarmed to realize I was joining in his laughter, dodging the spray and running.

I hadn't done anything this lighthearted in years and

years, not since my little brother and sister . . .

My memories swirled. I remembered them, almost heard them giggling with me through the sparkling water. I remembered, and for once, I wasn't sad.

I remembered, and I was happy.

I kept on running.

~

Winded, Harvey and I dropped onto the damp grass not far from the butterfly bush and tried to catch our breath. The scent of sweet blossoms and wet earth drifted by. I squeezed my hair, and he shoved a hand through his, spiking it like straw.

I wondered if he was as surprised as I was over what had just happened. Or was chasing someone with a garden hose normal behavior for him? Did he have brothers and sisters? Childhood friends?

He smiled sideways at me. "So in case you couldn't tell, I'm kinda competitive. And I totally won that water battle."

"Based on the fact that we're both soaking wet, I beg to differ." I glanced up at the sky. When had the sun climbed so high? "That was fun, but I should really get back to my studying."

"Yeah?" Harvey sounded genuinely interested. "What are you studying?"

"Entomology," I said, almost dreamily. I never tired of saying the word and picturing all it stood for. Maybe because I rarely had the opportunity to say it out loud.

"The study of words and their origins?"

My mouth quirked into a grin. "No, that's *etymology*.

Entomology is the study of insects. Etymology would probably be fun, too, but I like insects more than words. I think it's best to focus on earning one degree at a time."

He whistled. "Ambitious. So you have a class to get to?"

I laughed at the thought. "No, even better, it's right here, in my own home—or yard—depending where I bring my laptop. I'm studying online, learning at my own pace. I love it."

"Wow, that's cool." He tilted his head. "So. . . if it's at your own pace, you don't really need to go right now."

"Well, no, I don't *need* to, but I should. I haven't studied yet today, and I'm really looking forward to this next unit. It's all about Hymenoptera, which includes wasps, bees, and ants. . ." I rambled on for a little bit, detailing interesting facts until I realized what I was doing. "I'm boring you, aren't I?"

"Not at all. Who knew ants have two stomachs? Must come in mighty handy."

"It's not so they can eat like gluttons," I clarified. "One of the stomachs is actually a place to store food to share with the other ants in the colony."

"Nice. Glad I'm not an ant. Not that that's the tipping point or anything. I wouldn't want to be one for lots of reasons. Think about the chances of being stepped on. Not a great way to go."

"Oh, that wouldn't happen as easily as you think. You'd spend a lot of time underground."

"Well"—Harvey smirked—"that makes it so much

more appealing."

"Ha-ha. Well I think ants are fascinating. I was interested in them even before butterflies." I parted the grass and leaned close, searching for the busy little insects. "I used to spend hours just watching ants building their hills. Sometimes I'd feed them. I even had an ant farm once . . ."

There I went again. Who knew I could ramble like this? Perhaps that's what happened after so many years of not talking to people. I sat up. "Anyway, I should get back to studying. Shouldn't you be busy planning your wedding or something?"

"My—?" His brows drew together. "Oh, no." He laughed. "Heck, no. It's not my wedding." He appeared almost horrified at the thought. "The bride's special to me and all, but not like that. She's a relative. I didn't want to get her something off her registry, figured I'd get something a little more . . . creative."

"Butterflies."

"Yep."

A feeling, soft and shimmery as a gossamer-winged butterfly, flitted through me. I stood, wandered to the bush, and realized I hadn't even smelled the flowers yet. I leaned in for a quick whiff, then lingered in the irresistible scent.

Harvey appeared beside me, reached out, and snapped off a small blooming branch.

I eyed the broken twig, slightly concerned. The tiny bush didn't have many branches to spare. "Why'd you do that?"

"Don't worry, the bush'll be fine." He offered me

the blooming branch. "Bring it inside with you and put it in a glass. It should last a day or two. Your indoor butterflies might like it."

Slowly, careful to touch only the woody stem, not the delicate flowers, I accepted it.

I met his eyes and willed my voice to sound firm. "I'm not changing my mind about the butterflies."

"I hear you." He raised his hands in a gesture of surrender, yet I sensed he was nowhere near admitting defeat.

Taking a step back, he aimed his finger at me. "I'll leave you to your studying. Have fun."

I smiled and nodded. My hair brushed my neck, the strands already drying in the hot sun. "I will."

Though maybe not quite as much fun as I'd just had.

Chapter 4

Harvey popped into my mind at random times the next day, bringing a smile to my face as I swept my floor, watered potted plants, and edited butterfly pictures. But when I became absorbed in studying, I soon forgot all about him.

The next day, the same. He crossed my mind as I swept my porch and perused my yard for butterflies, but when I sat in a lawn chair with my laptop, intriguing insect data took over.

The pink butterfly bush lived up to its name and attracted the beautiful creatures frequently, affording me plenty of new photo ops and pictures, which I shared with Jess. And when we chatted online, the contrast to in-person conversation suddenly stood out to me. Her friendship had helped me through some tough times, yet something about our relationship was still lacking, still not quite as *real* as it could be.

Great pics. That butterfly bush new? she asked, ever astute to any change in my life.

It is. I hesitated over the letter *I* on my keyboard, then decided not to lie. I ended up with an ungrammatical fragment: *Planted it a couple days ago.*

Butterfly-man been back to bug you? A second later, an animated laughing emoticon appeared. Jess loved stupid puns.

Butterfly-man? I rolled my eyes. There was a nickname any guy would appreciate. Though perhaps not quite on par with butterfly recluse, it hovered in that realm.

Hello??????

My fingers started typing rapidly. *Sorry. Still busy groaning over your pitiful pun.*

You know you love 'em. So? Did the guy come back?

Once, I admitted. *The next day, still hoping to buy some butterflies.*

And?

I told him no, of course. My turn to insert an emoticon. I chose a smiley face.

～

The cutting from the butterfly bush became withered, the petals crunchy. I tossed it in the trash under my kitchen sink, then glanced out my window.

Something about the live shrub bursting with color brightened my spirits, and I was happy with my decision to plant it in that spot. It was perfect.

A monarch swooped down and sipped some nectar for lunch, and I gazed for a moment before preparing my own lunch, a simple ham and Swiss sandwich with a Bartlett pear on the side.

After my meal, I dropped my camera strap around my neck and headed outside in search of a new picture.

My goal each day was to snap at least one new image worthy of uploading to the stock-photo site. I made sales only sporadically, so it was a good thing I didn't have to rely on this income to pay bills. My home was mortgage-free, and my bank account was comfortable.

I wished it wasn't.

The price that had been paid to get here was much too high.

Shoving the grim thought away, I inhaled the fresh air and refocused my mind.

Photography was more my hobby than true work, but I was grateful for it. I loved sharing pictures of butterflies with the world, helping others appreciate their beauty. Any earnings were mere nectar in the flower, so to speak.

My lips twitching in amusement, I strolled down my long driveway while eying the trees on either side. Green summer leaves hung thick from the branches, twirling and flickering in the wind like thousands of jade butterfly wings.

At my mailbox, I kept my back to the road. When a roaring rumble approached out of nowhere, I snatched my mail and turned.

A motorcycle appeared around a bend moments before swooping to my side. The noise assaulted my eardrums, and I stepped back to my driveway, nerves firing.

The rider removed his helmet to reveal a familiar

grin. "Well, isn't this a coincidence?" Harvey yelled over the ferocious engine noise.

"It's not a coincidence. You know where I live, and—" And it was no use. I could barely hear my own voice. I shook my head and covered my ears.

"What? Too loud?" He cut the engine. "That better?"

A little.

His booted feet supported his weight while he remained on the bike. "Surprised to see me again?"

I found it difficult to focus on him with the motorcycle so close. Trying not to recoil, I swallowed. "Surprised you're still trying to convince me to sell you butterflies."

He studied me. "Will I get a different answer today?"

"Nope, sorry." I squared the envelopes in my hand, making all the edges even.

"Too soon, then, huh?" He tapped his helmet. "Figured I'd give you a few days to reconsider. But I'm running out of time here. Help a guy out."

I pushed the corners of the envelopes into my palm. "All you have to do is order a gift off the registry. Honestly, she'll like that. She wants those things."

"But she wants the butterflies more."

A trickle of sweat snaked down my back. "A few butterflies aren't going to make or break anything."

"A few, no. A few hundred, yes."

"You've got to be kidding."

He shrugged. "I dream big. Sally's worth it."

"Well, she must be. You sure are determined."

"I try." He set the bike's kickstand, then looped his

helmet on the handle and hopped to the ground. "That's quite a camera you've got. Mind if I check it out?"

I stepped back, protectiveness washing over me.

"Only if you don't mind," he added.

I hesitated. My Nikon was precious, but his request was reasonable. Sensing he'd be careful, I offered him the camera.

"Sweet." He looked it over, touching buttons, adjusting the lens. "This thing must take great pictures. Mind if I try one?"

"Go ahead."

He aimed the lens my way and snapped my picture without even a "say cheese" warning. I blushed and tucked my hair behind my ears. "Not me. It's for nature pictures, the trees, the sky, the flowers, the—"

"Butterflies. Right." He peered at the digital screen. "But look at that. Amazing. I took a picture of you, and it worked." He squinted. "I even—almost—got a smile." His brow lifted teasingly. "One more? A full smile this time?"

Flustered, I reached for the camera. As he playfully evaded my grasp, his fingers fumbled and my stomach lurched.

The camera dropped from his hands and crashed to the pavement—landing with a shattering sound.

Harvey sucked in a breath, then shot me an anxious glance.

"That's why I always wear the strap." I forced the words through strangled emotions and dropped to my knees, grief building.

I released my mail and retrieved the broken camera before tenderly turning it and examining the cracked lens. A jagged spiderweb of damage covered the entire surface.

An urge to cry swept over me, and when I spotted a scattering of rocks along the road, I wanted to pick them up and hurl them at Harvey's perfect bike, see how he liked it.

"Hey." His hand landed gently on my shoulder. "I-I'm really sorry."

I heaved in some air and made myself nod.

He spoke softly. "Can I take a look at it?"

Wasn't that how I'd gotten into this mess in the first place?

But it didn't really matter what he did with it now. I tipped the camera into his palms, feeling as if I were surrendering a piece of myself.

I waited, not knowing what for. Something inside me twisted and ached.

Harvey inspected the camera silently for a long minute. "I'll buy you a new one. An even better one. The memory card from this one is fine, so you didn't lose your pictures."

He looked at me, serious and concerned. "How does that sound?"

I snagged the corner of my lip between my teeth and bit down before answering. "I guess . . ."

"You don't have to wait for it, either. I'll take care of this today. It's the least I can do. I know a great place outside of town, Stewart's Cameras. They have the best."

He turned to his motorcycle. "Hop on, I'll take you there."

He had to be joking. "Right now? On—" I swept my gaze over the two-wheeled hunk of noisy metal—"on *that?*"

Chapter 5

"Sure." Harvey gave me a "why not?" look.

"No way." I shook my head. "I'm not comfortable with that."

"You'll be plenty comfortable. The seat's soft—"

"I mean I wouldn't feel safe."

"I know what you meant." His shadowed smile implied he thought I didn't know how to take a joke. Of course I did. This just wasn't the time or place.

He noticed my feet and cocked his head. "All you need to do is put on some shoes."

All I need to do is walk away.

He glanced back at the bike. "Know what? You're right. I don't have another helmet with me, anyway, so that plan won't work." He paused, his gaze lifting to meet mine. "I'm assuming you've got a car?"

"Yes, but . . ." I averted my eyes. "Right now's really not a good time. Or any time today, for that matter." I gathered the forgotten envelopes off the ground. "I have to sort my mail, start a load of laundry, and it's

Thursday, so I have to place my weekly grocery order."

Did I really just say all that out loud? It had never sounded so silly in my head. I should have simply said I needed to study.

But I was also thinking about how on Thursdays I always chatted with Jess at four o'clock sharp.

I glanced at Harvey warily, afraid to see pity. Or worse, ridicule.

But I couldn't read his expression. He stared, then moved till he stood by my side. He spoke over my shoulder. "One invitation from the Association of Retired Persons . . ."

My gaze snapped to the envelopes in my hands.

". . . one advertisement for an overrated credit card, and one from a dentist promising to fix your smile . . ."

I shielded the last piece of mail so he couldn't keep reading.

"Can't know for sure, but I think that last envelope wasn't any more pressing than the others. Just saying." He shrugged. "And as for fixing your smile, don't let anyone mess with it. The only thing that needs fixing is how often you use it." His strong gaze assessed me, warming me.

My lips pressed together, not knowing how to respond.

Harvey's boots crunched stray roadside gravel as he shifted his feet. "I thought a camera was important to you. Maybe I was wrong. I guess if you're that busy, I can just give you the money for a new one." He set the camera on the grass, then opened his wallet. "Again, I'm really sorry."

I inhaled in time to my beating heart. "Wait." I cleared my throat and swallowed. "I guess I could change my plans, if now is what works for you."

His furrowed brow smoothed. He closed his wallet, stuck it back in his pocket, and smiled.

"But we don't need to ride together," I added. "You take your bike, and I'll follow you." *No. Did I really just say that?* "How does that sound?"

"Sounds like a plan." He returned to his motorcycle and hoisted his helmet, as if making a toast to the sky. "I'll wait for you here."

~

I guess I'm going out into the great wide world. The thought needled me, disturbing my nerves. One just never knew what might happen out there . . .

I grabbed my purse, slipped on some flip-flops, and was about ready to leave when I caught a glimpse of myself in the hall mirror. Goodness, when had I last brushed my hair? It was honestly getting too long to care for properly. I paused to finger-comb my locks, then realized I probably shouldn't make Harvey wait.

But just the thought of following that motorcycle…

Get a grip, Lila. I opened my garage door and settled into my Honda Civic, my wonky pulse pounding. The car's interior smelled slightly musty. Since I hadn't driven in so long, I wasn't sure the engine would start. The internet, Amazon, and grocery delivery made it so easy for me to stay home indefinitely.

But I turned the key and the engine responded, so there went my last valid excuse for avoiding this chore.

After backing out, I turned around in my driveway and headed for the road. A huge part of me doubted I'd really find Harvey still waiting.

But, like a sturdy tree, there he was. Not only waiting, but smiling expectantly, as if this outing was something to enjoy.

The base of my neck prickled as he revved his motorcycle to life.

Here goes . . .

We zipped down roads, obeying the speed limit, yet the drive felt too fast. And the way he leaned his turns, the angle of his body to the road, ratcheted up my stress. My mind flashed horrible images of him wiping out, his body sprawling, my car hitting—

No!

I squeezed my eyes shut—not a good idea while driving. My lids shot back open, my heart hammering.

Maybe I should give up driving. It really wasn't necessary. The last place I'd gone was to church, and I had no intention of returning.

When Harvey finally pulled into the camera shop's parking lot, I doubted I'd be able to find my way back home. My phone GPS was useless without Wi-Fi, and I only had Wi-Fi at home.

I flinched when my door opened suddenly. Harvey stood there waiting for me, and I fumbled for my purse.

He inclined his chin in the direction of my passenger seat. "A Bible?"

Wishing he hadn't noticed, I didn't look at it. "It's been there a while."

Please don't ask.

Harvey stepped aside as I emerged, then closed the door behind me.

I felt his curious gaze on me, but I marched into the camera shop, determined to focus on cameras and nothing else.

One foot through the door, I froze, overwhelmed by the sheer number of incredible devices on display. I actually felt my fingers tingling and my mouth watering.

"Pick any one." Harvey's voice swelled with all the generosity of an indulgent Santa. "Price doesn't matter."

But it mattered to me, and I promised myself I wouldn't consider any camera worth more than the one he'd broken.

As I browsed the choices, I smothered my concern that, once again, Harvey was doing something kind for me, while I'd done nothing for him.

He had one simple, somewhat reasonable request, yet I refused to entertain it.

But I was justified, I assured myself. Some things just shouldn't be sold.

~

"You want that one, right?"

I did, very much, but I couldn't tell him that. It cost way more than the one he'd ruined.

"It's nice." I forced my gaze away to a lower-priced, sufficient model. "But so's this one." I made myself pick it up and assess it. "This will do."

"It'll do? Not quite what we're aiming for here." Harvey looked up and beckoned to the hovering salesman. "What can you tell us about the differences between these two cameras?"

I soaked in everything the salesman said, but when both men stared at me, waiting for my response, I had to speak. "It's too expensive."

Harvey shook his head. "I told you not to worry about that."

Still. "Mine didn't cost nearly this much."

"You have to allow for inflation."

I was pretty sure that didn't apply here, but I let it go, suddenly finding it difficult to argue with Harvey in front of an audience. And I was sure this audience, the salesman, was on Harvey's side. Probably earned commission.

Right on cue, the man cleared his throat. "Quality never comes cheap, miss. This camera will last you for years." He pointed at a red tag. "It's on sale through tomorrow, and you won't find it for a lower price anywhere."

"Hear that?" Harvey shot me a triumphant look. "It's a great deal. You can't argue with that." Still, he waited, giving me a chance to.

But I could see how much he wanted to buy it, the desire shining in his eyes, and I couldn't understand how he'd turned this into a situation where, if I said no, I'd be disappointing him.

The silence, the pressure of two people waiting for me, was too much.

"Okay," I finally agreed.

~

"Bet you can't wait to try it, hey?" Harvey asked with all the bounciness of a kid with a new toy.

"I'm looking forward to it," I admitted as we stood beside my car. Traffic whizzed past on the nearby highway. I held the camera close to me, almost as if cradling a baby. "Thanks again."

He waved my words away. "The least I could do. So where are you going to go to snap your first pictures?"

"Go? Well, home, of course. My garden will have plenty of butterflies."

Looking unimpressed, Harvey slouched against my car. "The same old spot with the same old butterflies? Why not go somewhere new?"

"I don't need to. I like my yard."

"Well, sure, it's really nice. But somewhere new might be nice, too."

He certainly liked trying to convince me of things. I almost told him he should go back inside the store and apply for a job, since he obviously had salesman blood in his veins.

"Come on, give the camera a chance to prove itself and break out of its comfort zone."

Sensing his odd metaphor actually referred to me, I chose to ignore it. I touched the camera case. "I'll take good care of it, don't worry."

"Oh, I won't, and I'm sure you will."

"Thanks again." I opened my car door.

He straightened. "You know your way home?"

Well . . . there was that little glitch. I sank into my seat. Both relieved and distressed by his question, I wasn't sure how to answer.

On the way here, my focus had been on him and his motorcycle, not the roads and landmarks. As a result, I wasn't confident I could find my way home without some serious guesswork—but to admit I couldn't would be like asking him for more help. Enough was enough.

"Um . . ." Harvey eyed me. "It was a pretty simple question." Despite the sarcastic words, he said them so kindly that it didn't sound rude.

His gaze prodded. "Should I take that as a no? It's no problem, just follow me. I've gotta head that way anyhow."

I pulled on my seat belt. "In that case, sure, that would be helpful. I-I don't get out this way very often."

And just like that, I found myself once again tailing him on his motorcycle, feeling as though the wind was actually rushing in my face and stealing my breath, despite my windshield.

I didn't even realize our route was different than the one we'd taken earlier until we swooped up a hill and turned past broken remains of a barn, a splintered fence, and an overgrown field stretching endlessly in front of us.

This wasn't my home. Where were we?

Other than the occasional car passing on a distant country road, we were alone. Isolated. My heart tripped over its own beat.

Why did he bring me here?

Chapter 6

I kept the engine running and sat with my foot heavy on the brake, not even shifting into park.

My gaze fluctuated from Harvey striding my way to the Bible on the seat beside me. *Lord, what's happening?* The prayer, feeble as it was, burst from my mind, catching me off guard.

My hand jumped from the steering wheel to the lock, where my finger hovered nervously.

Harvey tapped on the window. "Surprise." He smiled, but I didn't return the expression.

He tapped again. "Aren't you gonna get out?"

"Um, I don't know."

His knuckles rapped the glass. "What?"

I cracked the window a centimeter. "I said, 'I don't know.'"

"Why not?"

I shrugged, pretending my heart wasn't hitting overdrive. "Where are we?" I spoke to my windshield, focusing on a particularly nasty bug-splatter. "I'm just not sure—" That's when my eyes finally registered movement in the rolling field ahead. "Oh!"

Butterflies. Countless butterflies floating and flying, rising and settling in glorious abandon over hundreds of sunshine-bathed wildflowers. Purple, yellow, orange, and white petals bobbed over green leaves.

I could hardly tell where the flowers ended and the butterflies began. It was like one huge, living, intoxicating picture. More than a picture. It was real. The sight warmed my soul. I shut off the car and leaned closer to the windshield. "There's—there's so *many* of them!"

"A good place to try out that new camera, right?"

I scrambled for it, threw the strap over my neck, and unlocked the door. "I've never seen so many butterflies in one place. It's incredible."

Harvey laughed, then dodged my door as I swung it open. I heaved a lungful of flower-scented air and smiled as I hoisted the camera. "I've gotta go take some pictures."

I strode, almost ran, into the field, immersing myself in the rustling grass, the swaying coneflowers, daisies, snapdragons, and prairie clovers. The perfect blend of colors and scents soothed me. The intricate beauty delighted me. I savored the challenge and wonder of the shots until I stood breathless and beaming.

The pictures now sat like treasure in my camera, and I anticipated sifting through them for days. I finally let the Nikon hang from my neck and stood still in the waving sea of colors until my patience paid off and an exquisite swallowtail landed on my shoulder. Its wings fanned open and shut.

Harvey approached, and I felt a swell of delight that he could share this moment. "I hope you weren't bored," I said softly, grateful for his patience.

He shook his head, hair glinting in the late-afternoon sun. "Not at all." He waded through the long grass till he stood near enough to touch. The butterfly remained. As if it didn't know enough to be scared. Or maybe . . . it knew enough not to be. Strange emotions rippled through me.

"Thanks for bringing me here," I whispered. "It's wonderful. Magical."

He shrugged and smiled, almost sheepishly. "I knew you'd like it."

"I do." The butterfly crept to my neck, tickling my skin. Before I knew it, it was climbing my hair. I giggled, and it took flight.

Turning, I watched it sail away. "This place, it's like a . . . a paradise. A . . ."

"A butterfly heaven?"

I pulled in a sharp breath. "Exactly." But I wouldn't have expected him to come up with that.

His hands rose defensively. "That's Sally's name for it, not mine."

"Sally, as in Sally the bride-to-be?"

"Yep, my sister." He rubbed the back of his neck. "She loves butterflies."

"Right." Thus the desire for a butterfly release. He had a sister, and he seemed to know how special that was. The thought touched me. "Sally showed you this place?"

He nodded.

Confusion crept through me, along with something more complicated. "Then why . . . I don't understand. Then why did you think you needed me to provide butterflies? You could just come here and catch all you want." Not that I was condoning that. Although I was beginning to feel that the butterflies might understand, even forgive him . . .

He pushed his hands in his pockets and looked around, then down. Avoiding my eyes? "I think we both know I'm no good at catching butterflies."

"Well, sure. Without a net, no one is."

He laughed and shook his head. "I just wanted to do this the right way, that's all. And I thought you—that Sally would like it that way. That you would have butterflies you raised, ones that are ready for their first flight. These ones . . . well, they're already free."

He wasn't making a lot of sense. What wasn't he telling me?

He cleared his throat and looked past me. "Have you always been interested in butterflies?"

I shifted my thoughts, yanking them away from Harvey, away from Sally, away from freedom and weddings, and in doing so, I opened a door in my mind that had been shut and sealed for a very long time.

"Lila?"

What was his question? *Have you always been interested in butterflies?*

"No."

"So what got you started?"

Not what, *who*. "My little sister. She loved them first." Oh, Mags. She was like a butterfly herself. My eyelids weakened, lowered slightly, and my gaze turned inward, into my mind, into the distance, into the past...

"Do you think there are butterflies in heaven, Lila?"

"I don't know, Mags. How should I know?" I tapped my pencil tip against my math paper, irritated, before erasing the X in my equation.

"You should know because you're older." Mags hovered at my desk. "And you're super smart."

"If only," I muttered, then began recalculating. "Don't bother me right now. Can't you see I'm studying?" The ACT test loomed larger every day, along with college entrance exams and my desire to prove myself. A failed homeschooler would be the worst kind of label.

I couldn't let my parents down. I couldn't let myself down. My whole future depended on this.

Mags crawled under my desk, bumping my work, and I bit back a complaint as she continued chattering. "I think there have to be butterflies in heaven. They're too beautiful not to be. And I wouldn't want to go there otherwise . . ."

"I should have said yes," I whispered now through my oddly compressed throat. "I should have—"

A hand touched my arm. "Lila? What's wrong? I'm sorry, I must have said something—"

I shook my head and swallowed a lump, then batted my damp eyes, opening them to my surroundings. Realizing where I stood.

Butterfly heaven.

I inhaled and absorbed a warmth that had nothing to do with the summer air or sun. And I felt a closeness to Mags.

It's okay. She knows now. She knows . . .

Harvey stared at me with confusion and concern, his hand still on my arm, as if it belonged there.

Weakening, I sank to my knees in the deep grass, the green leafy walls swishing on all sides. If only they'd swallow me up.

Harvey sank beside me. "I'm sorry I brought it up, whatever it was."

I shook my head and smiled through the ache. "My little sister, she would have loved this place." I pulled in another breath, my nerves responding to the caress of the air. "I feel her here. I feel them all, my whole family."

I sensed Harvey's worried gaze on me, as if he realized what I hadn't yet said. I ran my palm lightly over the grass. "My mom, my dad, my little brother and sister—we were all really close." I pulled my hand back and hugged my knees. "They were my whole world."

Was I really doing this? Was I really talking about them? It terrified me, yet it made them feel real in a way they hadn't in years.

"My dad was a neurosurgeon. My mom homeschooled us. When my dad was home, it was special. One day, about five years ago, they wanted to take us all on a field trip."

Harvey gave a slight nod, still looking troubled.

"They were spontaneous and fun that way, but I—I had tunnel vision. I was focused on acing my ACT and college entrance exams. Always studying. Like it was all that mattered. Wouldn't even take a break to go with them."

I paused, drawing my hands together and tracing my knuckles, remembering the feel of the bitten pencil in my hand. Turning it. Matt's voice echoing Maggie's. *"Come on, Lila. Come with us. It'll be fun! We're gonna ride the zoo train."*

My eyes misted. "They really wanted me to come. I should have said yes. It was supposed to be family time. But I didn't want to, so they left without me and . . . I figured there'd always be more family time." I squeezed my eyes shut. "I figured wrong."

A heartbeat of silence pulsed between us before Harvey touched my back. "I'm sorry, Lila."

"They didn't even make it to the zoo. They swerved to avoid a—a motorcyclist who wiped out on the road." I swallowed, and when I spoke again, my voice rasped. "He died anyway, and their van was totaled." I willed the moisture to suck itself back into my eyes and nose, but no luck.

More silence.

"I should have been with them."

Harvey's hand left my back. He gripped my upper arms just shy of too tight, then looked me in the eyes, his expression somber. "No, don't say that. It's a good thing you weren't. A real good thing."

A good thing with no joy. "But I—I miss them. So much."

Harvey's brow twisted and knotted in a way that was difficult to watch. "Of course you do, Lila. Of course you do."

"And sometimes . . ." I paused as I felt our breath mingle, and it both delighted and frightened me, but I couldn't avoid it, his face was so near. How did it get so near? I looked at my lap and whispered, "I get tired of being alone."

His grip loosened, and I knew I shouldn't have let that slip out. What was I doing here, with him? I pulled myself from his grasp—easy to do. He didn't hold on.

I drank a breath of air to cool my burning chest and stood up. "At least I've got my butterflies." The silly statement and my chipper tone rang false.

Harvey's reaction resembled a grimace, producing lines near his mouth that didn't belong. "Lila, you have more than that. You don't have to be alone."

But I do. It's the only thing I know how to do. "Monarchs are in danger of going extinct. Did you know that? The population's gone down ninety percent in the last twenty years."

I popped the lens cap on my camera, then squinted up at the sky. "I think we should get going. I still have a lot of things to take care of at home, and I'm sure you"—my imagination fumbled in a million directions—"have things to do, too."

I hurried to my car and sealed myself in, scared by all the emotions I'd unleashed, the words I'd said. The weakness I'd revealed. The past I'd resurrected.

My gaze stayed down in my lap until I heard Harvey start his motorcycle, then I followed him onto the road.

I shouldn't have dumped my issues on him. I pulled in deep, rhythmic breaths, with equal exhales, all the way home, then jumped out before Harvey could reach my door.

I gave him a plastic smile, dismayed to see his anxious eyes rimmed with seriousness.

"Lila, listen—"

I shook my head. I was the one who'd gotten us into this emotional mess. Getting him out of it was the least I could do.

But before I found my voice, he was talking again. "What happened to you—to your family—that's a huge tragedy. You can't expect to deal with that all on your own. Have you tried counseling?"

Talk to a stranger about my personal issues? The mere thought brought my muscles to a gridlock. "That's not—that's not for me."

"How can you know that? Have you tried? My mom lost her best friend in a car crash, and she said talking to a counselor helped a lot—gave her a way to process and deal with it all."

I swallowed, my thoughts swarming and protesting. "I'm not your mom."

"Obviously." Sadness clouded his face. "I was only giving you an example."

I nodded. He meant well. I made myself focus on a too-long length of his hair that stood at an odd angle. "I'm sorry if I ruined your afternoon, but please don't worry about me." I eyed my door. Only a few more yards to go. "I'm good."

He hurried to stay near my side. "You're not, and I don't expect you to be."

Pretending he hadn't spoken, I knew what I needed

to say, and I just had to get it out. "Thanks for the camera, and for listening to me, but please—please go." I turned and strode up my path.

"Lila, wait."

But I didn't. I opened my door, slipped inside, and closed it. "Goodbye, Harvey."

Chapter 7

Other than when my family had died, my loneliness and loss had never felt so fresh, so acute.

I'd dealt with that by selling our family home, moving to a new town, hiding away and raising butterflies, immersing myself in my studies. I'd become relatively content.

But now . . . my simple pattern of existence had been disrupted, thrown off-kilter. Something had surfaced, demanding to be dealt with.

But I didn't know how.

I slipped into the sunroom, where there was no sun left. The butterflies hardly stirred, and the hidden pupas went through their slow metamorphoses inside cozy chrysalises. If only there was a chrysalis big enough for me to tuck myself into.

The silent room held a slight odor of molted leaves, potted earth, and perhaps a few caterpillar droppings. The butterfly-bath water needed changing. So did the fruit-juice sponges.

But instead of tackling chores or studying, I lay down on the area rug, willing at least one butterfly to care. To brush me and comfort me with a soft touch of wing. Just one.

But each insect continued hanging from the screen or resting on a plant, oblivious to me.

I closed my eyes and lay in the loneliness.

~

So what the heck, Lila? Where were you? Jess wrote hours later when I finally connected with her online. Not so much because I wanted to—goodness knows I didn't want to face her questions—but I didn't know what to do besides fall back into my old routines. It was the only comfort I could find.

After all, she was the only one who could truly relate. She'd lost her parents around the same time I had. Sadly, that was the main reason we'd connected so well all those years ago.

So today I'd dragged myself to my computer chair and found Jess waiting to unleash her concern.

Must've been some cataclysmic event to keep you from meeting me at our regularly scheduled time, she continued, unknowingly rekindling my pain.

How to respond?

It wasn't. It was just a little thing, really . . .

Yet my hands flew as I poured the day out through my fingertips, all of it: Harvey, my camera, the beautiful field, how I'd broken down and spilled my painful past.

I turned into such a mess, I finished.

Man, she replied, *that guy should just leave you alone.*

That was what she got out of this? *He didn't do anything wrong, Jess.*

He brought you to that place, made you talk about that stuff.

It was nice that he brought me there. He certainly didn't make me bring up my past. And maybe . . . maybe I need to talk about that, at least a little bit. Sometimes.

You know I'm here for you any time, Lila. Talk to me.

So I did. We typed back and forth till my wrists ached. Sharing was supposed to make me feel better, I thought, but it didn't.

Finally, I shoved my chair back from my computer desk. If anything, Jess's words further fueled my grief and pain. And I really just wanted to get past both, to get back to normal.

Or as close to normal as I could ever come.

~

Two full days passed before I brought myself to upload the pictures from the butterfly field, and much to my warring chagrin and delight, the images turned out even better than I'd expected.

I was absorbed in the process of enhancing one of the pictures when my doorbell rang.

After saving my work, I scooted away from my desk and crept to my front door, where I darted a covert glance through the edge of a window. I wasn't expecting any packages or groceries today.

My heart pounded, the opposite of what I wanted

it to do.

Harvey stood on my porch, looking as relaxed and nonchalant as if he belonged there.

He'd come back? After my embarrassing breakdown? My rude departure?

As I inched the door open, I practiced a cool, pleasant expression and stance.

"Lila, hey." He smiled. "I'm not interrupting laundry day, am I? 'Cause I know I can't compete with that."

I fought a smile and let my gaze slide past him to the sleek silver car in my driveway, which explained why I hadn't heard his bike.

Slipping a strand of hair behind my ear, I wondered what to say. Apologize? Ask him why he was here?

He shifted his hand and I caught sight of something resting in his cupped palm. A monarch butterfly.

My previous concerns fled. "How did you get that?" I stepped onto the porch for a better look and felt a pang of remorse when I saw that the left bottom wing hung ragged, broken.

My brows pushed together. "The poor thing can't fly. Do you know what happened to it?"

"No, I was just working on a motorcycle in my driveway when this guy flopped onto the grass a few feet away, trying to fly but only kinda hopping and, I don't know"—he scratched his jaw—"looking really frustrated, if you can believe that."

I could.

Harvey shook his head. "It's gotta stink to have a broken wing and not be able to do the thing you were meant to do."

"It'll adapt." *Poor thing, it doesn't have a choice.*

"Anyway, I figured you'd know what to do with him."

"Her."

"Her?"

I leaned in. The more I studied the butterfly, the more my voice softened. "It's a girl. You can tell by the black veins on the wings. Boys have a dot on the veins in each lower wing, about here." I pointed. "And girls don't."

"Oh." His forehead wrinkled. "Okay. Either way, I figured I'd bring it—her—here because I didn't think she'd survive very long on her own."

True. My heart twinged with regret.

"It's a shame." He moved his finger near the damaged wing as if he wanted to touch it but knew he shouldn't.

I drew the edge of my lip between my teeth, then released it. "So if it weren't for the butterfly, you wouldn't have come back?"

He looked at me, something guarded in his eyes. "Did you want me to?"

I broke eye contact and wondered how to reply. I watched him with the butterfly, his movements so careful, so caring. "I asked you first."

"Fair enough."

I waited.

"I don't know if I would've come back." His shoulder hitched. "On one hand, I hated leaving you so upset, but on the other, I figured coming back might make you more upset." He paused. "But when this butterfly flopped next to me and said, 'Take me to Lila,' I couldn't ignore it. Kinda seemed like a heaven-sent sign."

My heart faltered and I warded off a shiver. "The other day—that wasn't your fault. Not at all." It took everything in me to level my gaze at him. "I'm sorry if I made you think that. It was just the remembering and talking about my family. It—it threw me. I just needed some time alone."

"Sure, that makes sense." He sounded uncertain. "Do you need more time? Do you want me to go?"

"No, I'm glad you came back."

He looked relieved, then raised his palm. "So should we bring the butterfly inside? To your butterfly room?"

Into my sanctuary? I hadn't let anyone in there since . . .

I shook my head and caught the scent of blossoms on a breeze. "She'll like being outside better. I have plenty of flowers out here for her, and I'll bring her in later."

Something about seeing the butterfly nestled in his large callused palm—the clear contrast of tiny and delicate with big and strong—touched me. The only other man's hands I'd ever studied had been my father's, the skilled hands that saved lives. They just couldn't save his own.

"Come on." I led Harvey to a patch of marigolds, where he crouched on one knee and nudged the butterfly onto a flower. As soon as the monarch's feet touched the petals, her straw-tongue proboscis unrolled and prodded for nectar.

"Whoa, that's cool," Harvey said. "They can't bite with that thing, can they?"

I laughed, a refreshing release after the past couple of days. "You've gotta be kidding me. Are you serious?"

"Kinda." He cocked his head. "I mean, it sorta looks like a wicked little stabbing tool, a venomous needle."

I gaped. "Are you telling me you're afraid of butterflies?"

"Of course not." He looked insulted, but I suspected he was only pretending. "I picked it up, didn't I? Just don't ask me to pick up any spiders."

"Why not?"

"I don't like them."

"Really? I know girls who don't like spiders." Well, one girl anyway. Jess. She didn't even like typing about them. "But never any guys." Flawed logic, since I didn't know any other guys.

"Well, now you do. I don't like spiders, and I'm not afraid to admit it." His lip curled slightly. "But when you think about it, a butterfly's just a glorified spider with wings."

"It is *not*." I crossed my arms so firmly, I almost threw myself off balance. "In fact, there are so many differences that I don't even know where to begin. Butterflies have six legs, not eight, and butterflies are lepidoptera, not arachnids."

"Leopard doctor— What?"

I rolled my eyes and enunciated slowly. "Lepi-*dop*-ter-a. They can't bite, they can't spin webs, they don't eat bugs, and they aren't deceitful, hiding and waiting to take advantage of unsuspecting prey—"

"Okay, okay." He kept his eyes on the monarch, its wings opening and closing in a contented manner as it feasted. "Doesn't sound like you're much of a spider fan, either."

"Well, they wouldn't be my first choice for a pet, but I still find them fascinating. It's not their fault they're so sneaky. That's how they survive."

Harvey shifted on his feet and looked suddenly uncomfortable. He turned his full gaze onto me, which did funny things to my composure.

His mouth moved, but it took a moment for words to come. "I've been meaning to tell you something." He cleared his throat, and his obvious nervousness made me uneasy.

"About?" My toes scrunched themselves into tense mounds.

"About Sally—" His gaze caught mine, darted away, then returned, resolute.

Suddenly, somehow, I knew I wasn't going to like what he was about to say.

Chapter 8

Too bad I didn't have a chair to drop into. After glancing around, I settled for sinking onto my front step.

"Lila?"

"Go ahead." I tried to feign indifference, tried to stop my mind from racing.

"Okay, thanks." Harvey sat beside me and pulled in a heavy breath. "The butterflies were just an excuse."

He waited, as if that should mean something to me.

"An excuse? I don't understand. An excuse for what?"

He stared straight ahead. "The real reason I came here was to convince you to come to my sister's wedding, even if it was just me hiring you for a butterfly release. At least you'd be there. Because that's the best gift I could give her."

My eyebrows lifted. "Ever hear of something called a wedding invitation? Not that I'd want to go to some stranger's wedding—"

"That's just it." He rapped his knuckles against the step distractingly. "She's not a stranger. You met her when you first moved here. You were friends."

My lips parted, but he rushed on. "You met her at the grocery store, and from what she told me, you hit it off, started hanging out together. You even invited her over—"

"Wait—" My mind swam, a terrible thought surfacing. "You can't mean . . . not Sarah Sanford."

He nodded.

And just like that, it clicked. Sarah! Sneaky Sarah. Gossipy Sarah. How had I not suspected?

Because he was just as sneaky as his sister. Disappointment struck me. I turned on him with a frown. "Then why in the world were you calling her Sally?"

"I've always called her that," he said softly, almost apologetically. "Growing up, I had a real problem pronouncing r's. And even though it sounds old-fashioned, Sally's a legitimate nickname for Sarah. My grandma was the one who started me using it."

I thought about that for a second. "Harvey has an *r*."

"Exactly." His lip twitched. "I was known as *Hav*ey for years. I may never fully recover."

His amusement vanishing, he met me with a pleading look and returned to the topic I didn't want to discuss. "Sally feels terrible about what happened."

"She should." I jumped up, the memories slamming into me. She'd seemed so sweet, so kind and caring. She'd helped ease me out of my shell. I'd taken a risk by opening up to her and, most of all, allowing her into my home and my butterfly room.

"She took my grief and she—she turned it into gossip—turned me into a spectacle. She's the reason the whole town calls me the—you know." *The butterfly recluse.*

Harvey remained seated through my outburst, the epitome of calm, collected pity. "The whole town doesn't call you that. Do you think maybe you're exaggerating just a little?" He pinched his fingers a centimeter apart. "That's an awful lot of blame to put on one person."

My temperature rose and my face flushed. "That one person did an awful lot of damage."

"She talks too much." Harvey spread his hands. "Way too much, with no filter. It's always been her greatest fault. But she's got the best intentions, and she never meant to betray your trust or turn your story into entertainment. She just knows a lot of people, so when they asked questions about you, she probably said more than she should've. But she never said it spitefully, and what she didn't say, they probably filled in with their imaginations."

"Excuses. It's not that hard to keep your mouth shut. I do it all the time." *Before you came along, anyway.*

He laughed.

"This isn't funny." I aimed my finger at him.

"Lila." He said my name with such frustration, yet fondness, that it threw me. "You've gotta learn to laugh at yourself, at least once in a while."

I sniffed. "Seems I have enough people laughing at me without me adding to it."

"Sometimes, it's laugh or cry."

I blinked rapidly, closer to shutting down than crying.

"I wonder . . ." He drummed his fingers against his knee. "Don't take this the wrong way, but was Sally maybe an easy excuse for you to give up on the world?"

My mouth made ridiculous sputtering sounds. Not my finest moment.

"I get that things can feel overwhelming or that people can be difficult, but hiding doesn't change anything. You can't blame everything on her. Prove the gossips wrong, or at least—don't care so much about what others think."

Harvey stood and took my trembling hands. "You don't have to live hidden from the world."

"I *like* my world here." I swept my hand to indicate my home and yard. "I'm *content* in my world here."

He nodded. "I believe you. I just want you to know that there's more."

"You want me to forgive her."

"She's sorry, but you never gave her the chance to tell you. You cut her out of your life and she—" he gave half a grin—"she's not as persistent as me."

"No one is."

"Thank you."

Though some part of me liked the feel of his touch, I eased my hands away. "You should have told me you were her brother from the start."

"Maybe. But if I had, would you have talked to me?"

"Probably not." And what a shame that would have been.

His voice lowered. "She did send an invitation, by the way. When she didn't get the RSVP, she figured you were still mad at her."

And I was. *I am.* I blinked, vaguely recalling tossing away an envelope that had come in the mail from her.

"My sister's pretty tough, but that hurt her."

I stepped away, needing the distance, my mind muddled by his words, which made me out to be in the wrong if I didn't reach out and forgive.

But what if I didn't have it in me? How could I forgive her when I couldn't even forgive God?

And there it was, the deeper truth, the root of my pain: I still blamed God for what had happened to my family.

Harvey's eyes flickered compassion. "Life can be better, but you have to choose it. Don't throw away your friends. You don't have to be alone."

He glanced at the butterfly, which was no longer sipping nectar. It hung onto the flower in the sunshine, needing nothing more.

He gave it a nod. "Take care of little Glory—that's short for 'glorified spider,' by the way." He winked. "And I'll be back to check on her soon."

I barely blinked as he climbed into his car and disappeared down my driveway. But when I did, my eyelids forced a hot trickle of tears down my cheeks.

∼

You don't have to be alone.

What he'd said sounded so simple, but it wasn't. Allowing people back into my life would open me up

The Butterfly Recluse

to all sorts of disappointment and pain.

They'd all leave sooner or later. And with my luck, probably sooner.

I was used to living alone. I was okay with it.

Or I'd thought I was. Till Harvey came into my life and stirred everything up.

Inside my sunroom, I introduced Glory to Wingly. *Hello, nice to meet you. Let me show you around. It's not so bad living here.*

I settled Glory onto a milkweed plant and sighed. Why did I surround myself with butterflies? Why?

Because they were company. Safe, quiet, can't-hurt-me company. I wouldn't get a phone call out of the blue announcing they were all dead.

When one butterfly died or left, I had plenty more to transfer my affection to. And yet—by attempting to protect myself from pain, was I keeping myself from happiness?

My gaze wandering to the screen door, I reflected on my most recent happy moments—visiting the butterfly field, playing in the hose water, watching Harvey chase butterflies—and I groaned. All those moments included human interaction. And, specifically, they included Harvey.

Harvey, brother of Sarah-the-betrayer.

He'd asked me, very reasonably, to forgive her. But how did I even begin . . . ?

If my mother were still alive, I'd ask her. She'd always given the best advice, even if I seldom followed it. Her suggestions usually included some form of turning to God, and I didn't want to do that. I didn't feel like doing that.

Wants and feelings come and go, changeable as the wind.

My hands fisted. *I like the wind.*

But it can blow you off track. Think with your brain, not your emotions.

Where the thoughts came from, I wasn't sure. With a shudder, I wandered from the room and eventually found myself pacing near the garage door.

Why, God, why? Why did You take them? I still need them. I love them. I clutched my head. *I miss them.*

I sagged against the garage door, and it squeaked open. I stood and stared into the dimness at my car, fighting an urge that I didn't want to acknowledge.

At last, I gave in and retrieved my Bible from its banishment. I supposed it had sat out here long enough—since the last time I'd seen Sarah, at church, when I'd overheard the insensitive whispers and endured the strange looks.

The fact that she'd convinced me to go to church in the first place had been huge. After losing my family, my relationship with God had been strained, at best, but . . .

"You can do it, Lila," she'd said. "I know you want to. You just need someone by your side to help make it easier. I'll go with you. I'll even drive."

Highly uncomfortable with the entire idea, I considered it anyway, for her sake, and tried to show interest. "I'll think about it. But if I decide to go, I'll meet you there." That way, if it ended up being too much, too difficult, I could bail and drive home.

As if I could run away from God.

I didn't really intend to go, but I woke early on Sunday morning and, try as I did, I couldn't fall back asleep. No amount of tugging the covers over my head blocked the encroaching light or my thoughts. The day stretched ahead of me, my conscience prodding.

Scrounging every drop of courage, I showered and dressed, drove to church, and sat beside Sarah. I tried to talk to God, but never quite got there.

I kept feeling eyes on me, even thought I heard whispers, but told myself I was being overly aware.

Mentally exhausted by the time church ended, I was relieved that I'd made it through without fleeing.

Beside me in the pew, Sarah nudged me a little too hard, and I almost flinched.

"There's a big potluck brunch in the basement," she whispered. "Want to come with me and meet some of the people? You'll love them. And they always have the best donuts." She nudged me again. "Dibs on the sprinkled ones."

Her eyes twinkled with hope. I averted mine to the tips of my black, pinchy-toed shoes. "I'm kind of tired. Maybe next time?"

She patted my arm. "Sure. You did great today. This was huge." She walked me out to my car, gave me one of her smothering hugs, and trotted back to the door. "They better not have eaten all the sprinkled donuts!"

Smiling, I shook my head and watched her disappear. Then I stood beside my car, debating.

I glanced back at the church, at the side door that led

to the basement potluck. What if I did go? Would it really be that hard?

I should do it. I can do it. No one's stopping me but me.

At last, I straightened my skirt, smoothed my hair, and crossed the parking lot before I could lose my nerve.

Voices and laughter floated up as I descended the carpeted stairs. Maybe this was just what I needed, maybe this would be the start of—

One particularly loud, chatty voice hit me, and I paused halfway through the door.

"The way Sarah described her, I expected to see butterflies swarming around her."

"Or at least a few stuck in her hair."

Laughter made my stomach plunge.

"Not that you can blame the poor girl for going a little berserk after what happened to her."

The laughter faded.

"Yeah, if becoming some kind of butterfly recluse is what helps her deal . . . "

Elbows started poking and prodding, heads turned, and a few fingers pointed at me.

The only eyes I met were Sarah's, and the shock and guilt on her face pierced me more than all the careless words.

Because I knew she was responsible.

I fled up the stairs and out of the parking lot, leaving Sarah's friendship behind.

Now, standing on the cool concrete of my garage floor, the memory still hurt. The Bible sat heavy as a brick in my hands, and I didn't know what to do with it.

I'd blamed Sarah for driving me away from church, but the truth was, I knew she hadn't meant to be unkind. Like Harvey said, maybe I'd snapped up the excuse to not return there—or anywhere. I thought it would be easier, safer . . .

I don't know how to forgive anyone. Not Sarah . . . Not myself. Not God.

I wandered inside and settled at my desk with the Bible, staring at the cover for a long minute. My hand wavered.

Don't do it.

But I did. I opened the Bible.

I flipped quickly past the death-record page, where I'd written all the names of my family, all dated the same dreadful day. Ignoring the truth didn't change it. Maybe it was time I faced it.

I turned back to the death-record page and let my eyes linger over the ink strokes of each name, each one so dear and familiar.

Slowly, I touched my fingertips to the smooth paper, touched the next line, which was blank and ready for another name.

I should have been with you . . .

"*No, don't say that.*" Harvey's words intruded. He'd told me life could be better.

How? I asked. *Tell me how.*

But he wasn't here to tell me. There was no one here with me.

No one but God.

With a few clicks, I opened up a Bible concordance on my computer and entered the word *forgive*. A long row of Bible verses appeared, the word *forgive* highlighted in glaring yellow. I scanned them, my skepticism high.

For if you will forgive men their offenses, your heavenly Father will forgive you also your offenses.

The verse reminded me of the Our Father prayer, the one I hadn't said in so long.

. . . forgive us our trespasses, as we forgive those who trespass against us . . .

I returned to the computer screen and noticed a pattern of other words, ones like *have mercy* and *pray*.

Next, I typed in the word *friend*, and my eyes kept rereading one particular verse. *The good counsels of a friend are sweet to the soul.*

A wistful sigh escaped me. *Sweet to the soul?* Who wouldn't want that?

Maybe that explained the irresistible draw I felt in Harvey's presence.

I shook my head, knowing he was right. *Friends are important.*

But he wasn't the only one who'd been telling me that. Jess had been, too. I'd been holding her at a careful distance for years. And even though she'd wanted more, she'd stuck by me, settling for what little trust I gave her.

Moving my computer mouse, I opened a message to her, then wrote, *I've been thinking, Jess, and maybe it's time.*

I chewed on my bottom lip, and my brain sent the signal to keep typing. *Maybe we should finally meet . . .*

Chapter 9

A firm knock sounded at my front door. *No, no, no!* The timing couldn't have been worse. I was in the middle of mopping my kitchen floor and pretty sure I sported horrendous sweat patches beneath my armpits.

"Hold on, I'm coming!" I zipped past the front door and up the stairs to throw off my current T-shirt and pull on a clean one. As for my hair, well, there wasn't time. I slid a hand over it and galloped down the stairs to the door.

"You opened it." Harvey stood on my porch grinning as if I'd passed a life-changing test.

Maybe I had.

He'd said he'd be back, two days ago when he left me with Glory, and I'd believed him.

In my effort to forgive, I'd stopped replaying the church memory and replaced it with my first memory of Sarah and how we'd met, how I'd let her into my life in the first place.

Let her? I couldn't help a small smile. I'd let her in like I'd let Harvey in—unintentionally.

More like they'd burst their way in, with a brightness that wouldn't burn out.

Shortly after I'd moved to town, I'd driven to the grocery store because I hadn't started ordering groceries online yet.

I'd been distracted as I pulled into a parking spot, and a scraping sound startled me. Realizing I'd made contact with the car parked beside me, I groaned. I reversed and readjusted my car, though I wanted to flee.

But that wouldn't be right.

I emerged with a leaden stomach and eyed the damage on the Ford Fusion. Not as bad as I'd feared—barely a dent—but there was a noticeable scratch. Not something I could simply ignore.

I looked up and down the lot but didn't see anyone heading my way.

What to do?

After waiting a few moments in hopes the owner would appear, I dug a pen and paper from my purse and wrote my name and number, as well as a short note: *Sorry I scraped your car. Call me and I'll get my insurance to take care of it.*

Feeling slightly better, I stuck the paper under a windshield wiper.

"Hey, whatcha doin'?"

I turned to see a tall dark-haired young woman striding my way.

I straightened and tried not to mumble. "Is this your car?"

"Yep." She nodded, popped open the door, and grabbed her phone off the seat. "I forgot this. What's up? What's with the note?"

"I scraped your car when I was parking." I felt foolish admitting it. What kind of grownup didn't know how to park?

One who barely drove. One who was distracted by grief.

"Yeah?" She didn't sound worried. "Where?"

We rounded the car and I showed her, pointing out the black streak on the sapphire-blue paint.

"That?" She ran her fingers over it. I noticed the remains of chipped purple polish on her nails. "That's not bad. In fact, I bet my brother can fix that for me, no problem. He'll probably enjoy doing it, too, the weirdo." She shrugged. "So you did him a favor."

My spirits lifted slightly. "So you don't want my insurance to take care of it? Are you sure?"

"Oh yeah." She waved her hand and smiled. "I'm not gonna blow a gasket over something that tiny." She pocketed her phone. "You heading in?"

"Yeah, I was . . ."

We fell into step, and somehow she drew out the fact that I was new in town. She insisted on helping me shop, finding all the best deals for stocking my fridge, freezer, and pantry. And she practically made me buy a certain kind of donut, claiming that they were "to die for."

I never expected a grocery outing to be quite so much fun. It certainly took my mind off my problems.

Maybe I'd made a good choice moving to this town.

Not that I expected to see Sarah again, but she had my phone number from that note, and she invited me to meet up for lunch a couple of days later. And before I knew it, getting together with her became a regular thing.

And I realized I'd made a friend.

The memory, which I'd blocked from my mind, touched me now with guilt. She'd been so kind, so ready to forgive, and when my turn came, I'd refused. My stomach turned.

I hoped it wasn't too late to fix this.

Harvey had presented me with an opportunity, and now here he was. I couldn't help giving him a big smile.

My heart raced, but I told myself that was from running up and down the stairs.

Mostly, anyway.

"Friends," I blurted. "I mean, I'm willing to try being friends again with Sarah. I forgive her." I figured the first step was saying the words.

"Really? That's great, Lila. Thank you." He tilted his head. "And me? Do I get to be your friend, too?" He sounded teasing, playful.

My tongue almost tangled while trying to speak. "If you want to be." I felt a blush rising and turned away. "You probably came to check on Glory. I'll go get her."

I hesitated with the door half closed, suddenly caught in a quandary. I wasn't ready to let Harvey into my house. I had a lot of cleaning left to do before it would be guest-worthy, and . . . and I didn't let anyone in my house. "Wait on the porch. I'll be right back."

"No problem." Another smile.

That smile. So kind and caring. I closed the door and collected myself.

Moments later, I emerged with Glory in hand.

Harvey nodded. "She looks good, but I knew she would." His gaze didn't stay on her for long. "I knew you'd take great care of her. So now that we're friends, how about going for a walk with me?"

I reined in my skittering nerves. "You're not going to drop another truth-bomb on me, are you? No more sisters I need to forgive?" I transferred Glory to my other finger, but she wasn't content to stay in one spot. She crept on me like a spider.

"Nope, I promise, and no bombs. Actually, I was thinking you'd help me plan one to drop on Sally. Not a real bomb, obviously. I should probably stop using that word."

I laughed, suddenly encouraged by the simple fact that I wasn't the only one who stumbled over words. I wasn't perfect. Harvey wasn't perfect. Sarah wasn't perfect.

No one was, and life sure wasn't perfect—but it didn't mean we couldn't enjoy some perfect moments.

After I returned Glory to the sunroom, Harvey and I strolled along the road, walking farther than I'd ever ventured on my own. We crossed into a neighborhood lined with tall trees and meandering sidewalks.

"So now that you know the whole truth, I'm not going to bother you about the butterfly release anymore. I'm just going to ask you one thing, and you probably know what that is." Harvey glanced at me hopefully. "Will you go to the wedding?"

I was about to answer, when he hurried on. "I'll even drive you. Imagine how surprised Sally would be to see you. What do you say? If you need some time to think about it, that's fine, too."

I smiled at his obvious anxiety. In truth, I'd sensed this was coming and given it a lot of thought already. "I'll go." I'd do it for Sarah, and I'd do it for him. My friends.

Harvey let out a whoop. "All right! Thank you! And you'll have a great time, I promise."

I suspected he was right. Something about being near him seemed to bring good times.

Childish laughter floated toward us on the breeze, and I pointed ahead. "Look, a park." The place was in walking distance from my home, and I hadn't even known it. The flowers and colorful play equipment made the place look charming and inviting.

"I used to love bringing Mags and Matt to the park. They could play there for hours." My voice softened. "They were ten years younger than me, but when they were born, I was never jealous of them. Never. They always made everything better."

Harvey took my hand and squeezed it. "I bet you were a great big sister."

I felt my palm beating a pulse against his, warm and steady. Comforting. "I could've been better."

"Come on, we could all say that. I could've been a better brother too, but Sally's stuck with what she's got."

I laughed. "You don't seem that bad to me."

"Oh, we went at it something terrible growing up.

Once I was old enough to find out she used to make me play tea party and dolls with her—" He coughed. "Forget I said that. But yeah, she was the older, bossy sister, and I was the younger, obnoxious brother. But we always had each other's backs."

"Siblings are great that way."

We crossed onto the spongey, rubbery playground surface. "Look," I said, "there's even a merry-go-round here. Wow, those are hard to find these days. Guess they're not considered very safe anymore. But they were always Mags and Matt's favorite."

The metal merry-go-round base had been painted in multicolored wedges, like a pie. I sat down on a red one.

"Hold on." Harvey pushed one of the yellow rails, and I started whirling. He ran past me in a blur. Faster, faster. Colors flashed by, and I grew dizzy with laughter.

"Hey, mister!" a child's voice yelled. "Can we get on?" More childish voices echoed the request.

They obviously knew a good thing when they saw it. I tipped my head back and it bobbled. Suddenly I was surrounded by kids. More laughter, more fun. The grass and trees and sky zoomed by.

Finally, Harvey stepped back and leaned over, his hands on his thighs. "Whew. That's all I've got for now."

"Awww!" the kids moaned, but they quickly recovered, scattering to other play equipment.

"Did you like the ride?" Harvey took my arm and helped me off. Good thing. My legs wobbled, wonky as a newborn deer's.

"It was super fast."

"My motorcycle's faster." His tone held a hint of challenge.

"I don't doubt it."

"Slicing through the air, the wind ripping past—it's the greatest feeling. I'll never forget my first motorcycle ride."

Despite my spinning brain, I wanted to focus on his words. Spotting a swing set with two empty seats, I headed for them. "Let's sit."

I gripped the chains, kicked off my flip-flops, and skimmed the earth with my toes. "So what got you interested in motorcycles? Why do you like them so much?"

He laughed. "What's not to like? I've always loved them."

A memory of Matt playing with toy motorcycles blipped through my mind. He'd loved them, too. I could still hear the *vrroom* noise he used to make as he ran the motorcycles across the floor. Sometimes I got down on my hands and knees and raced him.

"I didn't save for a first car," Harvey said. "I saved for a motorcycle. Mowed a ton of lawns. My parents didn't like it, but they didn't stop me from buying one. Probably knew I would've anyway, somehow. But my dad took my keys away all the time, every excuse he got, till I finally moved out at eighteen."

He twisted on the swing to face me. "Don't get me wrong, he's an okay guy. We just didn't see eye to eye on a whole lot. He wanted me to be a doctor, but after high school I got this great chance to work at a motorcycle shop with the owner. Kinda like an apprenticeship. Now I build and repair motorcycles for a living, and I love it."

"'Choose a job you love, and you'll never have to work a day in your life,'" I quipped. "That's a saying from a little calendar my mom gave me. Not sure who first said it. I've always remembered it, though, and I totally agree with it."

A young family with three kids strolled past, and the mom gave us a second glance before approaching. "Excuse me, could you take our picture?"

Harvey looked at me and grinned. "Your specialty."

I sprang up from the swing. "Sure, I'd love to."

"Then I'll take yours," the mom promised.

And just like that, in mere moments, Harvey and I stood side by side near the park sign, and just before the woman snapped our picture, he put his arm around me.

Chapter 10

We had so much fun together, I typed to Jess that night, needing to relive what felt like the best day of my life in years.

We walked to a park, and we talked about all sorts of things—kinda like we do—and it wasn't as hard as I thought it would be. Harvey doesn't feel like a stranger anymore. Some family wanted me to take their picture for them, so I did, and then they took our picture.

Jess responded, *So show me!*

Smiling, I uploaded the photo for her, then gazed at it too.

You make a cute couple, she replied.

We're just friends.

For now, maybe.

Yet I knew Jess well enough to sense her unwritten thoughts. My fingers struck the keyboard harder than necessary. *You don't approve.*

Sorry, Lila. The last thing I want to do is burst your bubble, but he looks kind of cocky to me. I know the type, believe me.

I hovered the cursor over the sticking-out-my-tongue emoji, barely able to keep myself from clicking it.

Just be careful, Jess wrote. *Please. I don't want you to get hurt. I know you're all excited about this date, but—*

It's not a date. I couldn't type the words fast enough. *He never said it was a date. He asked me to the wedding as a surprise for his sister, that's all. She and I used to be friends, but we had a falling-out.*

I'd confided in Jess about it at the time, but now I hoped she didn't remember.

Is he picking you up? she asked. *Is he driving you?*

Yes.

So it's a date. I'm warning you, if he breaks your heart, I'm gonna stomp on his.

Deciding not to acknowledge that, I waited for her to type something worth replying to.

So when are we finally getting together? she asked.

Oh, in all the excitement, I'd almost forgotten my impulsive promise from two nights ago. *Soon! Definitely. Maybe after the wedding?*

I'm going to hold you to that. And here's hoping I'm not going to have to end up drying your tears.

Come on, I wrote, *be positive. Be happy for me. It's about time I made a friend.*

As long as that's what he is. Just remember, it was less than a week ago that the guy drove you to tears . . .

Stop twisting things, Jess. You know that's not what happened.

Our chat session wasn't nearly as fun as I'd anticipated, and as soon as I could manage, I signed off, preferring to guard my new friendship from Jess so she wouldn't overanalyze it.

~

We went for another walk the next day, then the next, and Harvey's pleasant company and our lively conversations became the highlight of my days.

Try as he might, though, Harvey couldn't convince me to accept his offer of a motorcycle ride. I respected his determination, but I didn't trust the hulking machine. Even though I knew how important motorcycles were to him, I couldn't bring myself to mount one.

He cruised into my driveway late one morning on a bike I'd never seen before. The red body complemented the shiny steel frame, all the curves and lines sleek, bold, and striking.

Harvey kicked the stand into place, dismounted, and strode to my side. "Hi, Lila. Will you do me a favor?"

I eyed the motorcycle. "No, I can't go for a ride."

He waved my words away. "One of these days. But that's not what I'm asking. I need somewhere to park this thing for a week or so, till after the wedding."

"Why?" From my understanding, he had a big garage large enough to house all his bikes and then some.

"Sally hangs around my place too much, since I'm such an awesome brother and all, and she's too perceptive. I don't want her figuring out my secret." He patted the bike as if it were a beautiful stallion. "Can you keep a secret?"

"Easily."

"Sally's been eyeing this baby for weeks. I'm gonna give it to her as a wedding gift."

Wow. "I thought *I* was your gift," I teased.

He smiled. "True, and you're gonna top this one, which is just kind of a bonus. I guess she'll have to let her husband use it too." His face brightened. "But who knows, maybe she'll be the one to finally convince you to take a ride."

"Dream on. And I'm sorry, but I don't have room for that thing in my garage."

"That's okay, I've got a weatherproof cover for it. If you'll just let me park it on the side of your house, behind those big bushes, that'd be perfect."

I tapped my foot a moment. "Okay." I supposed this was the kind of favor a friend would do for another.

"Great, thanks." He wheeled the bike out of sight and tucked it protectively under the cover. "Now, I know it'll be hard to control yourself, but try to resist the temptation to sneak in some wild rides."

I smothered a laugh. "Yeah, right."

"Everyone's got a little wild side to them." He crossed his arms. "Should've seen me at sixteen. I would've scared you."

"I don't think so." I couldn't imagine anything scary about him. Intriguing, yes. Headstrong, yes. Scary? No.

"I had a mohawk."

My jaw dropped. "No."

"Yep. I dyed it black, too." He ran a hand over his

pleasantly messy blond hair, which looked so right it felt wrong to even imagine the mohawk.

"My mom cried. My dad called me a disgrace, then didn't talk to me for a month. Sally loved it, though. She even dyed her hair blue and purple, her way of diverting the situation. She's loyal, and she'd do anything for me." He shrugged and glanced back at the bike. "So I figure maybe she's worth giving two gifts to."

If his intention was to warm me up to the idea of seeing Sarah again, he was succeeding.

"So what about you?" He crossed the driveway. "You never did anything crazy like that?"

I pretended to think hard, though I knew my answer was a resounding no. Not crazy like that, just odd like shutting myself away from the world with a bunch of butterflies for friends. But he already knew that.

"When I was twelve, I wanted to go to a slumber party so bad that I snuck out after my parents were sleeping."

He appeared slightly impressed. "Did you have fun?"

"No, actually. I felt so guilty, I couldn't enjoy a second of it. I finally called them. They were so relieved. They'd woken up and saw I was gone and were about to call the police."

"They must've been pretty worried."

"They were. What parent wouldn't be?"

"Sure. Yeah, of course." Harvey's forehead furrowed. "I can see that now, looking back. I guess I probably gave my parents more than their share of gray hairs. Though I'm not gonna take all the credit—Sally deserves a good chunk, too." He rubbed the back of his neck. "So were your parents mad? My dad would've flipped."

"They only grounded me for a couple of days. But I was so sorry I'd worried them like that, I thought they should've grounded me for at least a month."

"So hard on yourself, Lila."

"It all worked out. That pretty much squelched my rebellious desires." Thinking back on the past with a sad fondness, I added, "I had a good childhood."

I really did. And that was something to be grateful for, I realized.

Harvey tilted his head and looked at me strangely.

"What?"

"Nothing. I mean, something. Something about you. You're different from other girls I've known."

I laughed. "You're only just realizing that? I'll save you the wondering. I think it was the homeschooling."

His mouth shifted thoughtfully back and forth. "Maybe . . . But there's more to it than that."

~

Later that night, as I selected items to fill my virtual cart for my weekly grocery order, I searched boxes of hair dye just for fun.

I'd never go for a drastic color change like purple or blue, but I'd occasionally wondered what it would be like to be a redhead. Impulsively, I clicked on a box of "foxy red" and added it to my cart.

The next second, I took it out.

Click, back in it went.

Out again.

Honestly, Lila. I rolled my eyes and resumed shopping for produce.

But when my grocery order arrived the next day, I discovered that, somehow, the dye had ended up in my order after all.

A mistake, or a fortuitous coincidence?

Either way, I couldn't be bothered to return it to the store. After admiring the tresses of the beautiful model, I tucked the box away in the back of my bathroom shelf and forgot about it.

For a little while, anyway.

Chapter 11

Horrified, I clutched my head and dreaded opening my eyes to the mirror and the reflection I knew would still be there, the unfortunate truth I'd discovered too late: I didn't look good as a redhead.

With a moan, I wondered why I hadn't left well enough alone. Why had I given in to my impulsive urge to dye my hair right before the wedding? Because I thought it would be *fun*?

This was anything but fun.

My intention had been to look boldly beautiful, classy and majestic.

Not this.

Oh, this was awful.

Maybe it wasn't as bad as I thought. Screwing up my courage, I opened one eye.

Ugh, worse than before.

I raced to my computer to search for a way to return my hair to its former state. A terrible urgency tore at me. The wedding was only a few hours away.

~

Staring at the mirror, I feared I now had a legitimate excuse to remain a recluse.

A rap on the front door jolted me. I knew the sound of Harvey's knock well, but this time when it came, my nerves seized.

I didn't want anyone seeing me like this.

After shampooing and soaking my hair with lemon juice and vinegar, I'd bleached much of the offending color out, but not enough . . .

Something had gone wrong, and the method had only succeeded in transforming the color more than removing it.

Was there any chance people wouldn't notice?

Please, Lord? A prayer of vanity—I didn't expect it to be answered.

I tried not to wobble to the door. All that time fussing with my hair had depleted me of the chance to practice walking in my new shoes. What had possessed me to buy a pair with such high heels?

I opened the door, my heart hammering and my flimsy shawl sliding down my shoulders.

Harvey's lips smiled, but his eyes revealed surprise. His mouth opened slowly. "Your hair's . . . pink."

Yep, he definitely noticed.

I could tell he wanted details but was suddenly too polite to ask, his refined demeanor matching his attire. His tuxedo appeared to be tailor-made, more expensive than a month of groceries.

Despite how handsome he looked, I almost wished

for the familiarity of him in jeans and a T-shirt, which would've set me more at ease.

The grin never left his face. "You look great."

But would he tell me the truth if he hated my hair? Way to put him in an awkward spot, Lila.

"You'll go well with my mandatory"—he made air quotes—"*salmon*-colored tie."

I barely glanced at the tie as I touched a lock of my hair and wrapped it around my finger. "I'm really sorry. I didn't mean for it to turn out like this. I didn't mean to look like some kind of spectacle."

My gaze shifted to my lavender painted toenails peeking from my open-toed shoes, and it pained me to continue. "I'm probably way too inappropriate-looking for church now." My voice dropped. "I'll understand if you'd rather I stay home." Mentally, I was already debating which '50s movie to watch tonight.

"You kidding me? Of course not." He tilted my chin up, and the gentle touch sent a tingle through my jaw and down my spine. "You're not getting out of this that easily."

He stilled my hand, then released my twisted hair. "You're making a much bigger deal about this than it is. Really." His finger trailed down the side of my face. "You look beautiful."

My cheeks probably blushed the same shade as my hair, so I tilted my head from his view. "If you're sure. I mean, about me still going."

"Positive. On both counts." He stepped back. "It's not all pink, you know. More like pink highlights. Some girls pay major money for that, and you're telling me you did that yourself? If the entomology thing doesn't work out, you could make it big as a hair stylist."

I laughed. How did he always know just what to say?

"Now let's get moving. I promised Sally I'd be there as early as the rest of the guys."

Right, he was in the wedding party. I'd have a lot of time on my own today. I swallowed, then remembered something. I reached over and seized the handles of a mesh enclosure filled with over a dozen monarchs.

"Look." I hoisted the large, but light, container. "They just came out of their chrysalises this morning. Their wings are dry by now and they're ready to be released soon. Isn't that perfect timing?"

"Wow, so perfect that I think it was meant to be."

I liked the way he looked at me when he said that, as if he meant more than butterflies.

Friends, we're just friends. And that's a big enough step for me.

"It's not a few hundred like you wanted," I said. "It's not even one hundred."

"It's more than enough." He opened his car door and helped me slip inside. Compared to the outside heat, the interior felt wonderfully cool. I placed the butterflies and my elegant little purse near my feet, then clicked my seat belt into place.

"Mmm, your car smells nice." I'd never smelled anything quite like it before. "Like new leather and fresh laundry."

He chuckled. "Glad you like it. Feel free to take as many breaths as you want." He started the car and slid out of the driveway while I gathered my hair and shoved it over my shoulders, behind my neck, where I'd be less likely to see it. I'd curled it and tried to pin it up in numerous different ways, attempting to hide the pink, but no updo looked right, so I'd finally settled for a half-up, half-down style.

I shifted in my seat and adjusted my skirt. The fabric felt a little clingy. Should I have picked a different dress? Maybe one with more coverage. While there wasn't anything indecent about this one, I still felt exposed. I thought the shawl would help, but it was rather thin, and what if I got cold?

"You're gonna have a great time." Harvey smiled at me. "I promise."

I wanted to believe that, but there were too many unknowns for me to relax. Was this really a date, or not? Would I make a fool of myself somehow? Worse, would I embarrass Harvey?

"I'm sorry I'll be busy with the wedding party a lot of the time, but that's the price—I mean privilege—of being brother of the bride."

"Of course, no problem. I understand." But I was already thinking ahead to arrival and how I'd have to sit in the church by myself for at least an hour or two before the service began. The same church I'd been humiliated in and told myself I would never return to. Rather ironic. I squeezed my knuckles.

"You're welcome to stay in the car and read until the wedding starts if you'd be more comfortable that way."

Tempting, but no. I squared my shoulders. "No,

that's what a recluse would do, and I've decided I'm not going to be one anymore."

He gave me a glance, and I caught a glimmer of admiration. "Good, 'cause I actually don't have any books for you to read in here, anyway. Unless you count the car manual."

Funny guy. "I have a paperback in my purse."

That pulled his gaze from the road. "You do?"

"I mean, it's just a little one. In case of an emergency."

His brows arched in disbelief.

"A boredom emergency. What? That's a real thing." In my life, anyway. Not that I thought I'd ever be in danger of being bored with him, but I didn't know how much time, if any, we'd really be spending together. I was going to the wedding for Sarah, not for him, and I shouldn't forget that fact. I folded my arms and cupped my elbows. "I think I'll stop talking now."

Harvey laughed. "No, don't. It's very entertaining."

I slid him a look through narrow eyes, his good humor drawing a smile from me. A couple of butterflies fluttered in the enclosure as they readjusted their positions on the mesh walls.

The ones in my stomach fluttered too. "Okay." I decided to ask him something I'd been wondering. "How come I never met you back when I met Sarah?"

"Right? How rude of her not to introduce us."

"Seriously, Harvey. I never saw you around, not even at church."

"Maybe you just don't remember."

"I would," I insisted. "You're memorable."

His head swiveled my way with a smirk. "Thanks, so are you." He fiddled with the radio for a second, but didn't switch it on. "You didn't see me because I was away on a mission trip, to Peru."

"Wow, that sounds like . . ." *Like you have a huge heart that cares about others, and a good soul that loves God.* ". . . like a big commitment."

"It was only for two weeks. Did some chapel-building, helped some locals, that kind of thing. Wasn't nearly enough time for all that needed doing."

I looked at him with probably a little too much admiration.

He shook his head. "Don't start thinking that makes me some kind of great guy. I've got lots to make up for. I was reckless back in the day, not very considerate. Dated a new girl almost every week."

He rubbed his chin. "I won't tell you the names some people called me, though I probably deserved them. I liked having a good time—I mean, what I thought was a good time. It wasn't, not really. Used to make Sally so mad when I hooked up with her friends."

I nodded slightly, at a loss for words but feeling I needed to respond somehow.

Harvey made a right turn and we traveled past a tidy row of two-story houses before pausing at a stop sign. He glanced down both streets before moving forward. "I used to go to church for all the wrong reasons. Out of habit. And for the girls. The attention went to my head. Seemed like they all had their eyes on me."

"What, were you like the only guy at church?"

He chuckled. "Felt like it, but no." His tone

sobered. "The girls' parents sure didn't like me, not that I cared. Then one day I just stopped going to church altogether. I preferred sleeping in on Sundays, nowhere I had to be, no dressing up."

He was quiet for so long that I asked, "So what changed?"

A moment hummed between us before he spoke. "One Sunday, I was out for a ride on my bike, and I took a turn too sharp. Never even saw the loose gravel."

He paused, and my hand rose to my throat.

"I wiped out—flew off my bike and skidded across the road. I was a mess, barely conscious. Luckily someone came by and called for help."

I squeezed my eyes briefly and tried not to picture it, tried not to feel sick.

"But that fall, well, I guess it was what I needed to knock some sense into me."

He inclined his head. "An empty, shallow life, it isn't much of a life. And at the end of it—which I thought it was for me that day—that's not an end I want to face. Not alone. Not without God."

Clearing his throat, Harvey stared intently out the window. "So I came back. Got my priorities straight." He tapped the steering wheel. "God's real good at giving second chances. Third, fourth, and hundredth ones, too. Good thing, 'cause I screw up a lot."

He'd never sounded so serious. I tried to process everything he was and wasn't saying.

"So despite appearances, I'm actually not perfect." He winked. "But I'll admit I was once stupid enough to think I was."

He glanced at me, overly long. "I learned something else, too, laid up in a hospital bed for days. The girl I'd been seeing at the time couldn't even stand to look at me. In her defense, I looked terrible. Still, she couldn't wait to leave. She didn't say it, but I knew she was worried I'd stay ugly."

Harvey grinned, though the gesture seemed stiff and lacked humor. "She didn't want to be tied to that, to me—didn't realize I'd recover so well and so fast. She wasn't into me, as a person, but into my looks, my image. Made me wonder if I was shallow like that, too." He raked a hand through his hair. "Yeah, I think I learned a lot from that accident. What's real and worthwhile . . . what's not."

I tried not to be stunned. Tried to think of something to add to the conversation. All that baring of his soul, and all I could offer in return was feeble silence? It wasn't sufficient.

"You're not," I said. "Shallow, I mean. Not at all." My indignation blended with sadness, and I tossed my hair, no longer caring it was pink.

That girl he'd been with, she should have been so relieved he was alive—how could she have left his side? How hurtful. He deserved so much more.

And there was so much more I wanted to say. To assure him he was a good person, kind, loyal, determined . . . "You took a fall like that, and you still ride motorcycles?" I couldn't fathom it.

"Sure. It's like riding a horse. You gotta get back on, face your fear. Conquer it."

He was brave, too.

With a turn of the wheel, there we were, pulling into the newly sealed parking lot of the stone church. Slow as I was today at conversation, I still would have preferred to simply stay in the car, listening to Harvey talk.

He glanced at the time, then pocketed his phone and keys before exiting the car and opening my door. He retrieved his suit coat from a hanger in the back seat and slid his arms into it. "Way too hot for this thing."

The butterflies batted their wings, diverting my attention.

"I can't leave these out here in this heat." I grabbed the enclosure. "They'll have to come inside with me."

"Sure." Harvey nodded and walked. I followed, then scooted to his side, trying not to straggle behind. These heels were going to be a challenge.

"So this is where I leave you." He indicated the rear door of the building. "I have to wait in there with the guys. Bride's orders."

I swallowed, still processing his earlier words.

"You okay?" Harvey paused with one foot on the steps. "It's not too late. You can still wait in the car if you'd prefer."

"No, of course not. I'll wait in the church like I said. It's fine, no big deal. I want to. I was only . . ." *Be honest.*

"It's just . . ." I swapped the butterfly carrier to my other hand. "After everything you told me in the car, I was wondering if, because of all that . . ." I gave a stiff shrug and focused on the shadow cast by the church. Wished I was standing in it. Probably ten degrees cooler over there. The way I was perspiring right now, I could sure use some shade.

"Yeah?" he urged.

"So now . . . so now you don't date?"

There, I'd said it, and the ground hadn't even swallowed me up. Though I might soon wish it would. I'd said the words way too casually to actually sound casual.

Then—horrors—he hesitated. His foot slid off the step and returned to the ground as he leaned toward me. "So now . . . I'm very, very particular. In fact"—his voice dropped—"I only date girls with pink hair." He swooped a finger gently down one of my loose curls. "And pink faces. Ones that blush exactly that shade." He gave my curl the slightest tug. "What about you? Do you date?"

I almost laughed. "I think you know the answer."

"I'd like to hear it."

My gaze skittered sideways. "I . . . I might if I found the right guy."

"Yeah?" Half his mouth appeared to grin, while the other half seemed to hold in a secret. "And would you recognize him if you saw him?"

Chapter 12

Before I could manage an answer, Harvey simply smiled and disappeared through the door.

Just as well. The way my mind was spinning, I hadn't even come close to formulating a reply. Maybe I'd be able to by the reception. Or maybe we'd both forget about it by then.

I hoped he would.

I hoped he wouldn't.

What was this strange feeling swirling within me? I'd never felt this before. Almost in a daze, I missed the sidewalk, as if unable to follow a straight line, and rambled through the grass to the front door of the church.

Lightheaded, I slipped inside and settled on a wooden pew, and it took a few moments for me to realize I still clutched the butterfly carrier close to me. I hastily nestled it onto the floor, then knelt and tried to pray.

The wedding flowers and pew bows punctuated my

vision with rich bursts of color. The expansive church felt larger than I remembered, probably because it was so devoid of people.

I closed my eyes and rested my forehead against my folded hands. I kept picturing Harvey sprawled and injured on the side of the road. A car could have hit him, killed him. I shuddered.

Thanks for protecting him, Lord. He's special, really special. My lip twitched. *But You already know that, of course. You made him that way.*

I paused, uncertain how to continue, but then a thought flowed out with no prompting.

I'm sorry for how long it took me to come back to You, Lord. I missed You.

I hadn't realized how much until now.

Prayers soothed my nerves, fed my soul.

Time slid by and I barely noticed. The first notes of gentle organ music rippled through the air, and guests trickled in.

When someone slipped in beside me, I didn't turn, but I sensed him glance my way. I leaned over and inspected the butterflies, satisfied to see them clinging to mesh or sipping from the juice-saturated sponge. They'd soon be free to enjoy summer air and fresh flower nectar for the very first time.

In my peripheral vision, I noticed that the man beside me was looking at me oddly. The skin on the back of my neck prickled.

Without meaning to, I gave in and glanced at him.

His brows rose. "Yours?" He indicated the monarchs. "I've never seen that before."

"What, butterflies?"

"In church. In a cage."

"It's not a cage, it's a habitat." I slid a few slow centimeters away from him. The pew creaked loudly.

His brown eyes glinted with amusement. "You bring them everywhere you go?"

I produced a composed smile. "No, I brought them here for a butterfly release."

"Interesting." He glanced around and leaned nearer, lowering his voice. "You do those a lot?"

"No, this is a first. For a friend."

"Really? Well I'm glad I'm here to see it. How do you know Roger? I sure wouldn't have pegged him for a butterfly guy."

"Um . . ." I cocked my head slightly. "Who?"

"The groom. You're sitting on the groom's side of the church."

"Oh." The groom's side. *That's a thing?* "Oops," I whispered, "my bad." Did I use that expression right? I'd never said it to anyone before, only typed it occasionally in chats with Jess, copying her in an attempt to sound cool.

"I guess I'm on the wrong side. I'm actually Sarah's friend." It felt good to say, made it feel real, and a strange glow filled me. I glanced at the other side. "Maybe I should move."

"No, don't. No one will mind." He smiled, and I realized he was attractive, though in a very different way than Harvey—in a mellow, straight-A-student or young-professor way, with his striking dark hair groomed so I could see the comb marks. Not a shadow of facial hair marked his chin. I imagined he'd look particularly nice in glasses, though he wasn't wearing any.

Jess sometimes joked that my dream man was probably some kind of nerd. I could imagine this man being my type, yet he didn't interest me in the least.

I turned to the front of the church to see Harvey enter with the other groomsmen, and my heart flipped.

"Name's Jay, by the way, and I actually barely know the groom." He leaned closer, and I caught a whiff of peppermint.

Harvey usually smelled of grease and grass and dirt, but I preferred that.

Jay's peppermint scent teased my nostrils and made me realize the polite thing to do was to offer my name in return. "I'm Lila."

"Nice to meet you."

"You too." I straightened my posture and felt my spine bump against the hard pew back. I bowed my head and tried to refocus on God.

Jay eyed the butterflies again, mock concern flicking across his features. "You think you can manage to keep those guys quiet during the wedding? Because if you need any assistance, I'd be happy to help."

My only reply was a smile, and by the time the wedding march began, I felt comfortable with my pewmate beside me, while Harvey grinned at me from the front of the church.

Smiling back, I almost felt like I belonged.

∼

Sarah looked more beautiful than I remembered. As she glided down the aisle, it was as if her trailing train swept away my old grievances, and my mind recalibrated to the truth. She had a good heart, which shone from her face, and I'd always known that deep down. She'd simply been the excuse I'd needed to avoid church.

But everyone in this place . . . I glanced around . . . they were here to celebrate, worship, and give praise to God—not to ridicule and gossip. Maybe later they'd talk about me, but whatever. There were worse things than gossip.

Peace seeped into my soul, and it felt good there. My heart softened and warmed as I followed the service, glad I'd come.

Glad Harvey had asked me.

This was the start of something monumental for Sarah, a new life. And here I was, a part of it.

Near the end of the wedding, Jay leaned sideways and cleared his throat, pulling me from my thoughts. He pointed at the butterflies. "So when exactly do you release them?"

My meandering brainwaves snapped to attention. "Soon!" Grateful for the reminder, I grabbed the carrier handles and, as unobtrusively as possible, slid from the pew. Fortunately, I'd sat near the back.

I made my way outside and down the front steps. Then I turned and faced the church, ready and waiting, heart pounding, nerves firing. The butterflies fluttered, reacting to the warmth and sunshine. "Soon," I whispered to them, "soon."

Grand strains of organ music filtered out the windows

and burst from the doors as they opened wide and revealed Sarah beaming beside her new husband. The wedding party and guests streamed out behind them.

Showtime.

I pulled the enclosure's zipper, the tiny white teeth producing a steady *zhirr* until the flap hung loose. I flipped it back, expecting the butterflies to take flight and soar free.

Only they didn't.

Each and every monarch remained contentedly clinging to the mesh wall or the juice sponge, wings pulsing, soaking the sun, not sailing into it, passively observing the world, not joining it. Not realizing the vast, beautiful freedom that awaited them.

I crouched down, an action more difficult than I expected in heels. "Go on," I whispered urgently.

A receiving line formed and the guests greeted the happy couple, all oblivious to the special tribute that was supposed to be occurring.

I tapped the side of the mesh. "Go now, before it's too late!"

"And she talks to them, too." I heard the grin in his voice before I saw it on his face. Jay had abandoned the receiving line to join me. "Need a hand?"

I released a puff of frustration. "They're supposed to fly out."

"Hmm." He studied them. "Maybe they just need a little encouragement, a nudge to get them started."

I frowned. "Maybe, but—"

He reached for the opening.

"Wait!" I shielded the entrance, blocking him.

"They're fragile. Don't touch their wings." I offered my finger to one butterfly, and he climbed on, prickly feet gripping, and I lifted him out. A breeze ruffled his wings, and suddenly he was airborne. Orange-and-black waved a rapid goodbye as he sailed away.

"Quick!" The effect would be ruined if the butterflies left one by one. No one would even notice such a pitiful release.

But Jay was a step ahead, already coaxing butterflies aboard his fingers. He brought out two on each hand, and away they flew. I was right behind him with four more.

And so we worked in a fluid, well-timed sequence, as if we'd practiced. The butterflies somehow caught on—as did the guests, and the oohs and ahhs and exclamations of "Look at the butterflies!" assured me the release was finally successful.

Some of the monarchs even circled the wedding party and guests, showing off, or perhaps attracted by the bright colors, bouquets, and boutonnieres. Who knew? But at least the butterflies were appreciated, especially by the children. Some kids even scampered off to chase them.

I glimpsed Harvey, who wasn't watching the butterflies. He was watching me, giving me a nod and a thumbs up. I never would have guessed from our first meeting—when *he'd* run after butterflies—that I'd end up here with him.

He'd gotten his way after all.

"Oh wow, Lila? You came!"

A fragrant cloud of white satin and tulle engulfed me.

Sarah smelled of exotic flowers but hugged like a wrestler. "I can't believe you came. And with butterflies!"

She leaned back just enough to look me in the eye, and I noticed hers shimmering. "Do you have any idea how much this means to me?" Her words almost caught on a sob. "I've missed you!"

"I've missed you, too." *I really have.* I blinked rapidly, fighting emotion. "Congratulations! I'm so happy for you."

"Me too." She laughed. "Everything's perfect, just perfect." She beamed at Jay, whom I'd forgotten about. "And this must be your date. How wonderful. Oh, Lila, I'm so happy for you. You make the perfect couple."

My eyes widened, but Jay smiled, apparently too polite to correct a bride's blunder. I supposed it was my duty. I pulled in a breath. "Actually—"

But the maid of honor tugged Sarah away to speak to a grandmother or great-aunt or some other elderly relative who'd flown in from a faraway state, and Sarah sent us an enthusiastic wave, calling, "See you at the reception!"

Chapter 13

"I'm so sorry." Not really wanting to, I shifted my gaze to face Jay. "I—"

"Don't apologize." The corner of his mouth quirked, revealing the hint of a dimple. "I think she's on to something. I'd love to be your date to the reception. Besides"—he gave a conspiratorial smile—"we can't disappoint the bride on her wedding day, can we?"

Why did he have to put it like that? I tried not to stutter. "I'm flattered, really, but I came with someone."

"Oh?" Curiosity and mild surprise crossed his face. "Sorry, I didn't realize." He glanced around. "Where is he?"

My eyes searched too, willing Harvey to appear and prove me right. Not that I had to prove anything, but I didn't want Jay thinking I was brushing him off with a lie.

"He's in the wedding party. Brother of the bride, so he's busy with family and pictures and . . . other things."

I bent to retrieve the butterfly habitat, now empty, then performed the tricky twists required to reduce it into a flat, folded square. "But thanks so much for your help. I really appreciate it. They were being so stubborn, I was afraid I'd never get them out."

"I knew you would."

Harvey's voice made my head snap up. He stood at my side, his tie loosened, his jacket draped casually over his shoulder.

He smiled broadly. "If it were up to me, I would've just shaken the things out."

Appalled, I heard a gasp escape my throat.

This is your date? Jay's eyes seemed to question, and I really didn't like the fact that I felt I could read his thoughts. Disapproving. Judging. *You and him? I don't see it.* But he smiled politely and offered Harvey his hand. "Jay, nice to meet you."

"Harvey." He shook Jay's hand and released it just as quickly, turning back to me. "Hey, so listen. I guess I should've figured this all out beforehand, but about getting to the reception . . ." He glanced toward the road, and I spotted a long, sleek white limo parked at the curb, waiting.

Anticipation bloomed inside me.

Harvey cleared his throat. "I didn't realize I wouldn't be driving you."

"That's okay." Totally. I'd never ridden in a limo before, couldn't even imagine what it would be like, but it would be fun to find out.

Harvey glanced from me to the vehicle and rubbed the back of his neck. "I didn't mean to do this to you, to put you in this spot, but the limo only has room for the wedding party. And we have to make some pit stops for pictures."

"Okay."

"So I was hoping you could drive my car to the reception. It's not far, The Blue Spruce Hall. You could GPS it, and there's a card in my car with directions."

He touched my bare arm, sending a cool zing through me despite the hot day.

"Is that okay?"

I blinked, processing. What he was asking of me was small, simple, reasonable. Again, something one would happily do for a friend.

A warm breeze blew my skirt around my ankles and pulled at my twisted shawl. I reeled the fabric in and bunched it into a ball. "Sure." I smiled and held out my hand. "All I need is your keys."

"You're sure?"

"Of course."

"Awesome." His smile reflected relief, and I tried to absorb it to calm my pounding pulse.

"Thanks for everything. I'll see you at the reception." He gave me a quick wave, then left. Looking around, I realized even Jay had disappeared.

I squeezed the black-and-silver key fob as I returned to Harvey's car and climbed into the driver's seat. I shut the door and immediately appreciated the bubble of isolation, the silence and solitude.

But it wasn't *my* bubble, it was his—and an obviously pricey one at that. I ran my palm over the thick leather wheel, not relishing the thought of driving an unfamiliar vehicle. I drove so little as it was, and only in familiar territory. Harvey must really trust me, though, and that was something.

I picked up the reception card lying in the console and squinted at the low-quality map. GPS would be preferable, but . . . I scoured the car . . . I didn't see any GPS device, and Harvey hadn't used one to get here.

He probably meant I could use my phone, but I couldn't. I didn't have Wi-Fi here, only at home or in Wi-Fi hotspots.

I returned to the little map and studied it.

After ten minutes of adjusting and readjusting the seat and mirrors, I still didn't feel ready. With a highly sensitive foot, I backed out slowly and pulled onto the road, trying to make my route match the wispy black line on the map card.

The fuel gauge hovered near empty. Forced to seek a gas station, I took a slight detour.

I soon found a pump and inserted the gas nozzle, and the cost ratcheted up. Minutes later, with a clunk, the car finally stopped guzzling gas. I removed the nozzle and, too late, saw a drop of gasoline fall onto the front of my dress and spread to a nickel-sized stain.

I stared at the ugly splotch for too long, then came to the conclusion that there was nothing I could do but ignore it. Disappointment touched me. This wasn't the way I wanted to arrive at the reception.

For a moment, as I glided out of the station, I considered turning for home and the comfort of non-expectations. I didn't look forward to entering the reception as a lone punk-haired, gasoline-stained guest.

But Sarah and Harvey were both expecting me. I squinted against the glare of the lowering sun, then flipped down the car visor. My night out had hardly begun. *I can do this.*

For a second, I even considered tying my shawl around my waist to hide the gas stain, but that would probably look a little too odd, even for me.

Ick, I even smell *like gas.* Did the odor come from my dress, my fingers, or both? Not a nice perfume.

Numerous wrong turns later, I finally caught sight of The Blue Spruce Hall sign and sighed with relief. Only now, judging from the packed lot and the endless line of cars parked along the street, I was likely the last guest to arrive. I had quite a walk ahead of me.

My heels crunched against the road, and the back of my shoes rubbed my skin. To cheer myself, I imagined sprouting butterfly wings and flying the rest of the way.

Sweat trickled down my back and dampened my underarms. I sure hoped I wouldn't be making my grand entrance with the charming fragrance of eau de sweat 'n' gas.

I hesitated at the door, hearing the din of voices leaking through. I tilted my chin up, shook my hair back from my face, then tucked and smoothed unruly strands into place.

Here goes. Clutching at both my purse and my courage, I stepped through the doors and into the crowded room. Noise hit me like a physical onslaught, and my breathing quickened.

It sure would be nice if Harvey would saunter over right about now, but I couldn't even see him.

Warm though I was, the abundant air-conditioning quickly chilled me. I wrapped my shawl around me and held it tight.

Step by tiny step, I maneuvered through the people, unsure where I was headed. Were weddings normally this crowded? But what did I know of normal?

In all my twenty-three years, I'd never been immersed in such a crowd. Not even at my family's funeral.

I could barely think clearly. The cacophony of so many voices talking simultaneously just about shook the roof. I marveled at how any of these guests could hear each other. Maybe they were all talking, with no one listening.

The boisterous crowd jostled me past the bar, which was probably the loudest spot in the whole place. I craved a drink of water and didn't see any pitchers on the tables.

But battling to be heard at the bar wasn't worth it, I decided, not with the progress I'd made through the sea of bodies, not when I'd have to backtrack. What I needed most was to sit down.

But where?

All the tables looked occupied—if not by people, then claimed by jackets or purses. I didn't see place cards anywhere.

I wouldn't be sitting with Harvey, of course, since he'd be at the head table with the wedding party.

Concern crept through me. As a last-minute surprise guest, would there even be a seat for me?

Chapter 14

My relief at finding a free chair at a corner table soon gave way to realization that the spot may have been left vacant for a reason.

Despite the deafening voices surrounding us, the middle-aged woman to my right was determined to be heard—at the expense of my eardrums.

She introduced herself as Pearl, then leaned into my personal space until her lips practically kissed my ear.

I gripped the edge of my chair and restrained myself from pulling away. Her breath radiated a bizarre combination of chocolate and cheddar.

". . . and that's cousin Irene, who was actually born in two states. I kid you not. She was born on a bus traveling from Illinois to Wisconsin, and she entered this world right as it crossed the border."

Pearl's gaze darted to a different guest. "Oh, and over there in the orange shirt, that's Carl Rudders. He lives on a lake—in a house on stilts. Must have cost a pretty penny, but I'd just never be able to trust those stilts . . .

"Now Burk, he's different. Never know what he might be up to. Last I heard, he was hunting rattlesnakes out West..."

I nodded but ran my gaze around our table. The heavy man sitting beside Pearl kept his eyes on his phone. "My husband," she'd told me earlier, apparently not inclined to expand on his story.

Across from me, a stunning young couple sent each other flirty gazes and appeared to be in their own little world. A petite gray-haired woman sat to my left, looking one yawn away from falling asleep.

So maybe Pearl felt it was her duty to keep conversation flowing.

As for me, only my starving stomach spoke up. I felt it roar ferociously but couldn't hear it, making me suddenly thankful for the din of the room.

Worse than my hunger, though, was my thirst, which continued to increase. Tracing back the details of my day, I realized my last drink had been from my bathroom faucet this morning, shortly before Harvey had arrived. Over seven hours ago.

Glowing tea candles, folded linen napkins, and shiny silverware graced the table, but all the food waited to be served at a buffet island located tauntingly close to our table. All the beverages appeared to be served from the bar.

For wedding favors, delicate folded fans lay at each table setting. Interesting and unique. Like Sarah.

In between scanning for Harvey, I cast glances over my shoulder at the oddest dessert display I'd ever seen. Only a few yards away, a large board the size of a small door stood upright with three long rows of wooden pegs protruding from it. A colorful assortment of donuts hung over the pegs like fat hoops on a ring-toss game.

Sarah was obviously still quite a fan of donuts. I smiled while my empty stomach urged me to cross the short distance and grab one—or better yet, three or four.

Both my manners and my thirst stopped me. If I ventured into this crowd for anything, it would have to be for a glass of water. Donuts would only make me thirstier.

". . . and anyone would. Marybeth, though, never takes no for an answer . . ."

I gave another polite nod to Pearl, who still prattled on. I found myself studying her impeccably applied, yet not overdone, makeup. Her precisely lined lips and her clump-free mascara fascinated me. No smears or errant black specks in sight. I almost wished I could ask her to give me makeup lessons.

Then her words stopped, and that got my attention. Her gaze lifted above me, and a moment later, I felt a slight touch on my shoulder.

A whisper of breath tickled my ear.

"Excuse me, but you look like you could use a drink of water." Jay set a large glass, clinking with ice cubes, onto the tablecloth in front of me. "Am I right?"

So right, I was amazed. Even if he'd guessed I was thirsty, how had he known I wanted merely water and not alcohol, a kiddie cocktail, or soda?

"Yes, thank you." My words were probably too quiet for him to hear above the racket, but I couldn't bring myself to shout.

"You're very welcome." His hand rested on the back of my chair, and I admired how at ease he seemed. I could use a little of that self-assurance.

I raised the cool glass to my lips and swallowed gratefully. I envisioned a waterfall pouring down my throat and smashing into my very empty stomach.

Pearl wiggled her fingers, which were adorned with chunky rings. "And who might you be, young man?"

Wonder of wonders, she didn't already know? From the way she'd gone on and on, I'd thought she knew everyone here, as well as each guest's entire life story.

"I—"

"Hey, everyone, how're we all doing tonight?" the emcee boomed into his microphone.

Heads turned and the crowd responded with a whooping cheer.

"All right, that's what I like to hear! Let's get this party rolling. If everyone could please take their seats, let's turn our attention to the entrance, because it's time to welcome the bridal party!"

"Sorry," Jay mouthed. With an apologetic nod at both Pearl and me, he retreated into the crowd. I found myself slightly disappointed that he wasn't at our table.

Pearl's eyes lingered on me with a questioning glint. "Shouldn't your date be sitting here?"

Again with the assumptions? "He's not my date."

"No?" Her expression remained unconvinced. In fact, her eyes sparked with far too much interest, as if I were hiding some tantalizingly torrid love affair. The mere thought made me blush.

Pearl wriggled slightly in her seat. "Do you have a date?"

How to answer that? "I'm here with Harvey Sanford, the bride's brother. I mean, he brought me." Well, to the ceremony, anyway.

"Oh, Harvey? I know him."

No surprise there.

Her lips moved almost in a spasm, making me wonder if she had a story to tell but was trying not to.

If so, her lips won. "So hard to keep track of who that boy's dating. Like keeping track of the flavor-of-the-week." She giggled, then sobered. "Be careful, dear. He's broken lots of hearts. Why, just the other day, his aunt, my friend Bernice, told me . . ."

My ears buzzed as the emcee again called for attention.

Pearl wasn't distracted. ". . . and a man that good-looking? A crying shame." She seemed torn, as if she wanted to lower her voice but knew she couldn't do so and still be heard. "And if you ask me, that could only mean one of two things, if you get my drift . . ."

I didn't, but I was afraid she was going to tell me.

Thankfully, guests stood and cheered as the grand march began. Bursts of applause punctuated the wacky, audacious display of groomsmen and bridesmaids making peculiar entrances that I wouldn't even know how to perform—odd dance moves, strange gyrations...

"Please welcome Harvey Sanford, brother of the bride."

At last, there he was.

". . . and Amber Blake, friend of the bride."

The beautiful blond bridesmaid leapt onto Harvey's back.

Unfazed, he proceeded to carry her—piggyback style—through the room to the head table, laughing.

Pearl poked my arm. "Are you okay? You look a little flushed."

I put a hand to my cheek. "I'm just really hungry, that's all."

"Sure you are." She sighed. "Well, I have to admit, even with all the rumors about him, I can see why you'd want Harvey over the water boy, too." She patted her heart. "Just don't get hurt, dear."

"Rumors aren't always true," I said quietly.

After Sarah and Roger entered to loud cheers, mine included, I sank back into my seat.

The head table, strung with twinkly white lights, felt far away. The inconvenient angle prevented me from seeing much of Sarah or Harvey.

I folded my hands and bowed my head for the blessing, then the bride and groom began the buffet line.

A string of speeches followed, first from the father of the bride, then the best man, and finally, the maid of honor. All paid tribute to Sarah and Roger's marriage, all making love sound lofty and magnificent.

Ours was the last table granted permission to visit the buffet island. Sarah and Roger had already cut and shared their celebratory slice from a one-layer wedding cake, a dessert so small that I hadn't noticed it earlier. No need for a tiered tower when you had a smorgasbord of donuts available.

Hungry as I'd been, I appreciated my meal of creamy

beef tips, crinkled red-skin potatoes, crisp green beans, fresh salad, and golden dinner rolls—a meal larger and finer than I'd ever made for myself. It reminded me of my mom's homemade meals.

"You look finished, dear," Pearl said. "Why don't you do our table a favor and slip over to that dessert buffet and bring us all back some lovely donuts?" She patted my hand. "That way we won't have to all go shoving our way through the crowd, and you're so slender it'll be no trouble at all for you."

Load up on sweets for this entire table of strangers? The thought appalled me. I wanted to say no, but Pearl's strong personality pushed me, and I found myself filling two dessert plates, stacking random donuts and feeling like I was being viewed as a greedy pig as I toted back the sugary heap.

When I set the donuts in the middle of the table for everyone, I was rewarded with a critical look from the pretty young woman across from me, who couldn't have heard a word of Pearl's request.

I may not have been familiar with reading body language, but hers said, *Excuse me? You think I want to eat those donuts after your fingers were all over them?*

I imagined I almost heard a sniff of indignation. She whispered something to her date and he chuckled as his gaze bounced off me.

At least Pearl's husband had no qualms about claiming three donuts immediately.

I looked down at my hands, sticky from sugar glaze, then reached for a napkin.

The lights dimmed. A love song began, and the bride and groom shared their first dance, so poignant my throat ached.

Chapter 15

"And now for the father-daughter dance," the emcee announced.

Sarah and her dad embraced, and the song began.

As if the previous dance hadn't tugged enough at my heart-strings, this one just about snapped them in two. Not just the song and lyrics, which certainly pulled my emotions, but the blazing, irreversible thought that even if I did someday marry, I'd never be able to share a father-daughter dance with my dad. Our tender moments were all in the past. And there weren't even enough of them as it was.

To my dismay, my eyes began leaking. I shifted my gaze to the tabletop dusted with donut crumbs and sporting a greasy stain from one of my errant, buttery green beans. Eating in front of an audience wasn't something I was used to, and being overly conscious of my every move and every bite had made my hand unsteady.

Now, pretending to dab at my mouth with my linen

napkin, I actually swiped quickly at my cheeks, removing any trace of tears.

I eyed the folded fan resting beside the crumbs. When I opened it, the delicate paper spread like a large white butterfly wing, one accented with tiny blue flowers.

I lifted the fan and appreciated its wide cover while I collected myself behind its comforting shade. The perfect shield.

Moving my wrist slightly created a refreshing breeze, and I lingered in it before closing the fan and setting it back on the table.

What to do now? Maybe I'd take a cue from Pearl's husband and focus on my phone for the rest of the night. Even if I didn't have any Wi-Fi, nobody else would know that.

Instead, with a deep breath, I stood, deciding to stretch my legs and slip to the bathroom and freshen up.

"There you are."

I looked up to see Harvey standing in front of me. The room's shadows flattered him, bringing out the angles of his features in a striking, mysterious way.

He smiled. "Why were you so hard to find?"

"Was I? I've been here all night."

"Glad I finally tracked you down. What's a guy gotta do to get a dance with you?"

I felt myself blush. "Asking would be a good start."

"Yeah? Okay, I'm asking. What do you say?"

The music thumped, the beat heavy, bold. "I'd like to, but I don't know how to dance. Homeschooled, remember?"

He scratched his head. "And your point is?"

Wasn't it obvious? "Normal kids learn how to dance. In high school, at school dances."

He laughed. "That's not dancing, that's just moving as crazy as you can. They don't give lessons, if that's what you think. And 'normal' kids? Come on, Lila." He nudged my shoulder, the contact causing a pleasant current to rush up my neck.

"You're not the only one who was ever homeschooled. And if you'd seen the kids I went to high school with, you wouldn't call them normal. Heck, you wouldn't call me normal."

My lips twitched. "I never did."

"Good." He glanced at the dance floor several paces away and started bopping his head and shoulders in a ridiculous way. "You saying you can't manage this?" His feet barely moved, but his arms and body sure did.

"Maybe." My brows rose. "Whether or not I *want* to make that kind of a spectacle of myself is another matter."

He shook his head, exaggerated disappointment covering his face. "I gotta tell ya, I wouldn't have thought a little dancing would scare a girl with pink hair."

"Pink highlights," I corrected. "And this isn't about being scared."

"Then what is it about? Come on, Lila. Be *norrr-mal*," he drawled, gyrating his arms, then shaking his hands. "All the cool kids are doing it."

"You're making this less appealing by the second." Yet his next moves made me giggle. He danced backward, closer to the dance floor, motioning me to follow.

Though I fought the urge, my feet inched forward.

"That's right." He nodded, his hair bouncing. "All you really gotta do is move. Feel the music. It'll tell you what to do. No thinking required."

Self-consciously, I quirked my shoulders, then my arms. Soon I was moving a little more, relaxing a little more.

Harvey's big grin and thumbs-up were apparently all the encouragement I needed.

"Yeah, you got this!"

Once I began ignoring how silly I felt, my muscles loosened and my arms swung freely.

"So do you wish you'd learned this in homeschool?" Harvey asked.

"No, I guess not."

If I had, he wouldn't have needed to teach me.

"I think homeschool would've been fun. Did you just hang out in your pajamas all day and watch TV?"

"Are you kidding me? My day was so structured, I'll never forget the routine. We had to be up by seven thirty. After breakfast, I had chores, and school started at eight thirty. First religion class, then math, then English. Science and history were after lunch." I ticked subjects off on my fingers, almost forgetting to dance as I gave him more details than he probably wanted.

"And yes, I had homework after school, even though it was all technically 'home' work. My mom was usually busy with my younger brother and sister, so I did a lot of self-teaching from books. I went at my own pace, and I liked that. I liked learning . . ."

Stop, Lila, just stop. Lamest dance conversation ever.

But it was all I knew to talk about. The music seemed to blare extra loud, with harsh guitar riffs.

"This singer sounds angry," I yelled over the man's voice. Tuning in to the lyrics, I wondered if I'd heard correctly. Something about "pink"?

I breathed heavily, suddenly very warm. Harvey danced closer and sweat trickled down his temple. The lights pulsed madly. His fingers tossed a lock of my hair. "It's 'Pretty in Pink.'" He moved even closer.

My mind glitched, and my uncoordinated dance moves made my heels wobble. I bumped into a stranger, then stumbled back, losing a shoe and giving the song a very ungraceful finish.

Harvey reached to steady me, but I ducked for my shoe, embarrassed. "I'm fine." I hopped on one foot and stuck my toes back into my shoe.

His eyes twinkled. "Your feet really don't like shoes, do they? Why don't you just take them off and dance without them? Lots of girls do."

"Really?" I glanced around, saw it was true. How wonderful. How freeing. I kicked them off at the edge of the dance floor.

Harvey laughed. "Biggest smile I've seen on you yet."

The next song was much easier to dance to, slow and soothing. He held me in his arms, and I seemed to fit perfectly. The closeness resembled a hug, something I hadn't shared with anyone in a long time, and I nestled into it, enjoying the pleasant sensation.

My feet, unencumbered, followed his lead and soon knew what to do.

Harvey didn't smell of the outdoors today, but like fresh linen and a hint of cologne. Without my heels to elevate me, my cheek rested near his jaw. His chin brushed me with a slight prickle, reminding me of butterfly feet.

Closing my eyes slightly, I imagined I was in an old movie, in a ballroom scene. Not a black-and-white one, though. In beautiful, panoramic Technicolor—that was the only thing that could do this moment justice.

My gaze wandered the room, not really seeing anything but vague impressions of colors and lights. We turned slowly, our steps meandering. Harvey didn't try any fast twirls or dips. He simply held my hand and my back. Warmth flowed in the slender space between us.

"You have beautiful eyes."

His random compliment made my heart flutter. "Thank you. So do you. I mean, they're really blue."

"Your eyes are like you, bright and interesting and unique."

Our eyes met. Something unspoken trembled in the air between us, an appreciation and admiration for what the other had brought into our lives. At least, that's how I felt. His zest for life, his kindness and consideration. All seemed to give him an inner glow that radiated from his gaze and drew me in. I'd never felt I belonged so well anywhere as right here, in his arms.

"What did you do when you weren't busy with school?" Harvey asked. "Like in the summer. You didn't have school all year round, did you? That would be horrible."

I laughed. "No, it wouldn't."

"Speak for yourself. My dad always made me take summer school. I hated it."

"Why?"

"It was indoors. Isn't that reason enough?"

"True, the best part of summer is being outside. Though I really liked spending time in the library, too. I once found a book called *Insect Pets*, and I was so excited. I felt like it was written just for me. But when I got it home, I realized it was actually called *Insect Pests*—and filled with ways to exterminate the poor things." I shuddered.

"The nerve of some authors," Harvey said, obviously trying not to laugh. "Guess you should have stuck to playing outside."

"Oh, I still did plenty of that. I actually had a lot of freedom in the summer. I hung out with my friends, went swimming, rode bikes. Sometimes we put on plays."

"Yeah? What kind of plays? That sounds a little too much like work to me."

"Fairy tales." I sighed dreamily. "*Sleeping Beauty*, *Snow White*, *Cinderella*. But the best one was *The Princess and the Pea*. We stacked a bunch of old sofa cushions a mile high and made this huge, tippy tower."

Distracted by the memory, I missed a dance step and glanced down at our feet. "Actually, I don't think we even ended up performing that one. It was too much fun playing with all the cushions."

My brother and sister, about three at the time, had squealed with delight at the sight, eager to get in on the action. I'd tried to stop them at first, to save the integrity of the play, but finally gave in and let them have their fun.

"It sure would've been something to know you as a kid," Harvey said. "Though you probably wouldn't have liked me. I probably would've sabotaged your play. I was never very good at taking direction. Wasn't a fan of fairy tales, either. So unrealistic."

"They're not supposed to be realistic. That's what makes them so refreshing."

"Except when they make girls grow up with unrealistic expectations, imagining they're gonna find some perfect guy who'll swoop in and save them from all their problems. No one can live up to that."

My lips parted, paused. "So you don't believe in happily ever afters?"

"Not the fairy-tale kind, where as soon as the guy and girl get together, they never have to work at anything ever again. Real people are too complicated for that."

"I agree that people are complicated, but—" Past Harvey's shoulder, I caught sight of a child running off with my heels. "Oh!" I pulled my head back and broke off our dance. "Some kid just took my shoes."

"What?"

"Over there."

He followed my gaze. "Want me to go get them?"

"No, keep dancing, I'll do it. I mean, not that I really need them right now or anything, but I don't want to lose them." They were the only heels I owned.

I trotted off into the crowd, warm and breathless, yet looking forward to returning to Harvey.

"Excuse me, excuse me." I wove past Pearl, strangers, and even caught sight of Jay chatting with an elderly woman. He caught my eye and gave a wave. I smiled and returned it but hurried past.

Within a few minutes, I tracked my shoes down to a girl of about seven wearing a sparkly blue dress. She paraded up and down the edge of the room with bold steps. She almost walked better in the heels than I did.

She spotted me watching her. "Are these your shoes?"

"They are."

"They're really pretty. The prettiest ones here." She swished her skirt. "I was gonna put them back. Are you mad? You don't look mad."

"It's okay," I assured her. "I'm not mad." She reminded me a little of Mags. "Have fun with them as long as you want. Just set them on that seat when you're done, okay?" I pointed to my chair, where my purse lay.

She nodded. "Okay, thanks!"

I glanced back at the dance floor, didn't see Harvey, and decided to run to the restroom before returning to find him.

Inside the echoey room, I heard a voice ring out from one of the stalls. "Obviously that's what it takes to turn his head these days. Gotta get me some of that pink hair dye."

Laughter bounced from another stall.

"It still won't be enough. Poor girl, do you think she has any idea he'll be done with her after tonight?"

My ears rang. A flushing toilet prevented me from

hearing a reply. I hurried to a sink and turned on the water.

A stall door rattled, then opened, and I ducked my head.

Someone approached, then stood beside me. I smelled a strong synthetic perfume.

"So I guess you heard us . . . sorry about that."

They knew who I was from my hair, of course. I turned off the faucet and glanced up.

"Some timing, girl. Your ears must've been burning." The second girl smirked and didn't look quite as apologetic as the first.

I cleared my throat. "Harvey's a nice guy."

"Well, sure, nice to look at," the first girl said.

"*Real* nice to look at," the second girl added. "And fun to dance with, among other things. But no one holds his attention for long." She eyed my hair. "No matter how hard they try." She turned and washed her hands.

I almost told her my hair color was the result of an accident, but decided I didn't need to justify myself. I lifted my chin. "You know all this from personal experience?"

The first girl shifted her gaze, then soaped and rinsed her hands. "Well, no, but people talk, and—"

"And it ain't pretty, darlin'," finished the other girl.

"Gossip never is." My shoulders tense, I walked toward a stall.

"Enjoy him while it lasts, because he'll get tired of you," the second girl said. "He always does. Everyone knows he's a player." She shrugged and pulled open the door. "But that doesn't stop most girls from wanting to play."

The other girl followed her friend but touched my arm briefly, kindly, first. "It's better to know."

A few minutes later, I emerged reluctantly, not quite sure what to think. I could only base my perception of Harvey on what I'd experienced, and it told me to trust him, to believe him—not the gossip. But what if I was being naive?

I headed for the dance floor, debating whether to share with him what I'd just heard, when I caught sight of him dancing.

I had told him to keep dancing, after all.

Only now . . . he was dancing with another girl, one of the bridesmaids—Amber—the one whom he'd very happily given a piggyback ride to.

He wore his widest smile, the one that lit up his entire face.

But they weren't carrying on to the sounds of a goofy, bouncy tune. This was a smooth, romantic slow song. Probably fairly easy to dance to—although Amber radiated self-confidence and probably could have nailed a tango.

Now she was in his arms, laughing, talking—and *not*, I was fairly certain, about homeschool or plays. They made a nice pair, with their golden hair and skilled dance moves.

I tore my gaze away and turned around, heading back to my empty, crumb-sprinkled table. I rubbed my forehead. The music made me dizzy.

This whole evening is making me dizzy.

In my corner seat, I smoothed my skirt. I opened and closed the paper fan, then tapped it against the table, conflicted.

Harvey could dance with anyone he wanted, of course. I had no claim on him and shouldn't think I did. Yet I'd begun to believe something special—even more special than friendship—had been forming between us.

Unless . . . had the talk about fairy tales been a type of warning, his way of telling me to ease off, back off? Was I coming off as needy? Clingy?

I hadn't thought so. I'd thought we were having a wonderful time tonight. I wasn't ready for it to end, but I didn't know how to get it back, or if I should even try. I certainly couldn't imagine myself walking up to him and trying to cut in on his dance. That would be too rude.

My mother had done a good job of raising me.

Maybe too good.

I set the fan down.

Suddenly inordinately thankful for my glass of water, I lifted it and downed a mouthful. The liquid pooled heavily in my stomach, and by the time I was done drinking, the glass was empty.

Chapter 16

I busied myself counting the individual twinkly lights framing the windows. It beat overthinking.

I'd reached eighty-nine when I decided I deserved another donut. And this time I was going to enjoy it. I was at a celebration, and this night was about Sarah, not me—and not about her brother.

I would find the most sinfully fattening donut there was, and then I'd take two. One for now, and one for tomorrow morning (if I could manage to cram it discreetly in my purse), when I'd look back at this night and laugh.

Okay, maybe not laugh, but I'd force a smile or two.

As I studied the remaining array of donuts, I realized I'd need another glass of water to wash the food down, so I followed the perimeter of the room until I neared the bar, which was crowded with groomsmen, their backs to me.

I immediately recognized Harvey's voice. Loud. Confident.

". . . lame pink embarrassment. What was she thinking?"

Laughter erupted from the whole group.

Pink? I touched my hair. *No, it's a coincidence.* He wouldn't—he couldn't be talking about me. Not after he'd assure me I looked fine. More than fine.

And the way he'd touched my hair and said *"Pretty in Pink,"* I'd thought that might have meant something.

". . . only did it for Sally," he went on. "But after tonight, goodbye and good riddance."

My mouth went dry.

". . . and every time she talks . . ."

My ears strained.

". . . I have to pretend to be interested. So glad it's almost over."

A groomsman thumped Harvey's back. "You're a great actor, man."

They laughed and fist-bumped. The other guys hooted and raised their glasses.

Appalled, I inched back and turned away. What I really wanted to do was yell, chuck my heels at Harvey, smack his mouth till it stopped laughing.

He's just lucky I don't make public scenes.

I fumed, anger consuming me. *But just wait. He still has to drive me home, and when he does, I'll—*

I'll—

I wasn't sure what I'd do, not yet. I was too upset to think, but I'd come up with something.

Something to make him feel what I was feeling right now. The humiliation. The pain.

He'd manipulated my feelings and used me all along.

How could anyone be so cold and calculating and . . .

My shoulders slumped. Retracing the past, I kept seeing him in my mind . . . in the car, at the park, at the butterfly field, at my house . . . sweet and considerate. How could it have all been an act?

I'd never admit it, but he deserved an Oscar.

Followed by a slap across the face.

I rubbed my temples, a headache building, and paced near a wall.

"Need another glass of water?"

I turned to see Jay offering me exactly what I'd forgotten I needed.

"Don't take this the wrong way, but you look like you could use a cool drink."

I reached for the glass, but he pulled it toward his chest. "Hold on one sec." He lifted a finger, and his eyes glinted with amusement. "You're not going to throw it at me, are you?"

"Of course not." I caught myself just shy of snapping.

"Because with the vibe you're giving off—"

"I don't give off vibes."

"Really? Then why do I feel one telling me to 'Get lost'?"

"Sorry." I blew out a puff of air, then pulled in a long breath, trying to collect myself—and my *vibe*. "You're not the one I'm mad at."

"Good, just checking." He handed me the glass, and I downed half of it.

I met his eyes. "Thank you."

"No problem." He made no move to leave. "So . . .

want to tell me what's bothering you?"

I rotated the glass, which chilled my fingers. He looked as cool and crisp in his suit as he had earlier. I averted my eyes. "No, not really."

He motioned to the dance floor, which had thinned slightly over the past half hour. "Care to dance?"

It was a nice offer, from a nice man. I almost wished I could say yes. "Sorry, but no. I'm actually here with someone." I'd told him that earlier, but now the statement felt like a lie.

Why was I clinging to some misplaced sense of loyalty? Harvey didn't deserve it. I was only hurting myself, drawing out the inevitable disappointment by clinging to false hope.

Jay glanced around, as if pointing out that I was *not* with anyone. But instead of humiliating me further by asking who or where my date was, he shrugged. "It's just a dance."

I nodded, and when I recognized the first gentle notes of a lovely old song, I relented. I set my glass on a random table. "Okay, sure. Why not?"

Why not, indeed? He wasn't the one who'd just made fun of me in front of a bar full of guys. I let him lead me out to the floor, and when he drew me into position, guiding me with one hand at my waist, I found the closeness strange, yet pleasant, a comfortable assurance that here in this moment, I was respected, cared for.

He wasn't laughing at me.

He moved with small steps, and I mirrored him. The swaying motion settled me.

His eyes smiled. "So tell me about yourself, Lila. Where'd you go to school?"

You've got to be kidding me. Not that subject again. Couldn't we just dance? The singer's voice should be the only one allowed right now.

"I was homeschooled." I braced for his reaction, but he didn't falter a step. In fact, he twirled me, and surprisingly, my feet kept up.

"No kidding? So was I."

I gaped. "You?"

"Yep." He tilted his head. "You sound surprised."

"A little."

He dipped me, making my stomach flip. His eyes moved close, as if peering into my soul.

I caught my breath. "Okay, a lot."

"Yeah? Why?"

"I haven't met many other homeschoolers, so I guess I assumed they'd be . . . different." *Like me.*

He laughed, then groaned. "You mean shy, awkward, socially inept, naive, sheltered, blah, blah, blah…"

His smile grew wider by the second, as if he enjoyed reciting the laundry list of dreaded qualities.

"Hey"—he touched my chin—"you don't really believe all that bologna, do you?"

"Ha." I lifted a finger. "There, right there. I'm pretty sure non-homeschoolers don't use the expression *bologna.* Unless they're like . . . ninety years old, maybe."

He shrugged. "I don't care what others think. Do you?"

I bit my lip. "Sometimes." I paused, suddenly feeling

I could ask him anything. "Do you watch classic TV and movies, too?"

"That might depend on your definition of classic. I like the *Rocky* movies, *Karate Kid, The Godfather.* Paul Newman, Clint Eastwood. So yeah, I guess so."

"Do you like board games?"

His eyebrows danced. "I play a mean game of chess."

I remembered playing chess with my dad. He'd never needed more than a minute to make his move, but some of mine took forever. He'd been so patient with me.

"You?" Jay asked.

I nodded.

"Sounds like we have some good things in common. Small world, hey?"

I shook my head. I understood the expression, but that was just it—it wasn't a small world. Not really. Not outside my home. Out here, it was a great big, scary world, littered with deceit and cruelty, a world I didn't feel equipped to handle. So I tried to make it small. *And that will never work.*

Jay angled his head like he was waiting for me to reply.

How could I explain what I was thinking? Did I even want to? Would he understand? "The world feels too big to me. Sometimes I wonder if that's because I was homeschooled." Or maybe, in my current state of mind, I was just playing the blame game.

"If you'd gone to public school, you'd be wondering something else. Like why you had to spend most of your childhood away from your family, battling peer pressure, being forced to learn at an average pace."

"Maybe I naturally learn at an average pace."

"Ha, I don't believe it. But at least you had the option either way. Me, I'm glad I wasn't institutionalized."

"Institutionalized?"

"Sure, that's what public school kids are. They practically grow up in government institutions."

"Isn't that kind of a harsh label?"

"No harsher than how they label us."

"Maybe no one should be labeling anyone."

"True, but people do."

We danced, not speaking for a few moments. He twirled me again.

I tried to keep up. "How'd you learn to dance?"

"Here and there. Watching, trying." He shrugged like it was no big deal. "You?"

"Oh, I didn't."

He glanced at my feet, his eyes glinting amusement. "No? What do you call what you're doing right now? My imagination? Because I didn't dream you up. You're too real. Even with all that homeschool, my imagination's not that good."

Such flattery. I brushed it aside. If I'd learned anything today, it was not to believe a man's compliments. "I mean, I'm learning to dance tonight. Now. You're a good teacher." Better than Harvey. The thought sent a pang through my heart. I almost turned my head to search for him, but stopped myself.

"Let me guess." Jay studied me. "I bet your parents homeschooled you for religious reasons."

I stumbled. How did he know?

"Relax, I mean that as a compliment. I can tell you're nice, that's all. I had religion, too. The way I see it, we were lucky. We learned to order our lives around God and family instead of peer pressure."

His sudden mention of God surprised me, yet it didn't.

"I'm glad I had the freedom and flexibility to explore my interests, shape my own future," he said. "I saw the world being big as a good thing, an exciting thing. Homeschoolers are self-motivated, and out of necessity we develop some rockin' independent study habits, am I right?"

"Well . . . wow." Dancing wasn't the only thing making me breathless now. "You got all that from homeschool? Maybe I should have gone to your house."

"I wish you had." He spun me again and the lights whirled. His tone deepened. "So you don't agree with me?"

"I'm just saying, homeschool is no guarantee of success."

"There aren't any guarantees in life, but some choices are still clearly better than others."

My gaze slid past his shoulder. "I think it's a bit . . . arrogant to assume we're better than kids who weren't homeschooled. They might have gotten comparable benefits, in different ways. I think most parents try to do their best by their kids."

"Sure, I didn't mean—"

"And weren't you ever lonely? Didn't you ever feel

different? Weird?"

"Whoa . . . I'm thinking I should really be insulted right now—"

"I'm sorry, that came out wrong."

"No, don't apologize." His smile revealed he wasn't offended. "We're unique, that's all. Unique doesn't have to mean weird."

Unique doesn't have to mean weird. I liked the sound of that.

"Everyone feels lonely sometimes," he said. "I wouldn't blame it on homeschool."

I wasn't, not really. I'd had friends through those years.

"I sure hope you give homeschool some credit," he added. "Because it seems to me that you turned out pretty great."

I ducked my head slightly.

He tipped my chin back up with a finger. "Hey, I mean it. Don't ever let anyone tell you differently."

∼

I had no idea how many songs we danced to. Certainly more than I expected. Somehow, Jay's company and conversation made time melt away.

"Lila!" Sarah appeared at my side in a rustle of satin. "There you are! Come on, you've gotta dance with me before the night's over!"

My focus popped, and I glanced around the room and remembered where I was.

I barely managed to wave goodbye to Jay before Sarah swept me off to the center of the dance floor, bopping and rocking to the pulsing music, her dress a wild flurry of white. Attempting to imitate her moves proved difficult when I couldn't see her feet. *Just feel the music. It'll tell you what to do.*

"So are you having fun?" Sarah's arms shot high, as if she were riding a roller coaster.

"Yes." I nodded, smiled big, and tried to believe it.

"So how long have you and your date been together? Will there be wedding bells for you next?" Sarah wiggled her brows along with her entire body.

It was all I could do to keep dancing. "Ah, no." I glanced back and couldn't even see Jay. "He's not my date. We only met today."

"Really?" Her jaw dropped, hanging lower than her long, dangly earrings. "You were totally hitting it off. You both looked really into each other."

I worked a shrug into my tired shoulders, and my ears felt like they needed to be unplugged. "We were just talking." How I'd been able to tune out this racket to have such an intense conversation with him was beyond me.

"Not just talking. Dancing slow and close, as if you were the only two in the room." She giggled.

"We had to be close so we could hear each other."

"Sure, sure. Oh, before I forget . . ." Sarah sashayed sideways down the dance floor, beckoning me to follow. She snaked out an arm and caught a groomsman by the elbow. "It's about time you meet my brother."

Chapter 17

My stockinged heels slid to a halt. My eyes met Harvey's and I felt a highly charged current of energy flash between us.

He still hadn't told his sister he'd met me. No surprise, considering his deceit and the words I'd overheard earlier, but the disregard still stung.

I lifted my head, trying to peer down my nose at him. But without the extra height from my shoes, I couldn't make it work.

I settled for a dry tone. "Oh, we've met."

"You have? That's great! Isn't he the best?" Sarah punched his arm.

I wanted to do the same. Only harder. Much harder. "The best."

"So where'd you meet? Here, tonight?"

"No." I tapped my toes against the ground. "Weeks ago."

Harvey frowned. Not with his face, just with his eyes. And just at me.

"What? And you didn't tell me?" She whacked his arm again.

"Surprise, Sis." He spoke to her but still looked at me. "Here she is, the friend you thought you'd lost for good—I convinced her to come. That's my wedding gift, so don't expect any fancy dishes or overpriced vases."

Just like that, he'd reduced me to the level of a knickknack, a useless something to stick in a cupboard and forget about.

"Yeah, that's me, the gift. Too bad he forgot to put me in a box, wrap me in paper, and top me with a bow."

"A bow might have been a bit much. You'd probably look kinda odd."

"No odder than I already look."

With smiles securely in place, Harvey and I eyed each other, our silence crackling with tension.

Sarah blinked and glanced from me to Harvey and back again. I saw this from my peripheral vision and assumed she was perplexed, but I wasn't about to break my stare-down with Harvey.

"Okay." She held up her hands, perfect French manicure flashing. "You're both weird, we know that. That's one reason I wanted you to meet. But you're also a couple of my favorite people—apart from my husband, of course. So we are dancing this night away together, hear me?" And she yanked us both out onto the floor.

Once I recovered my balance, I summoned all my energy and shimmied and shook and pumped my arms hard, all to keep from smacking Harvey when he ventured too close—which he seemed to be trying to avoid. In fact, he seemed to be trying to keep Sarah between us as a shield. Smart guy.

Cowardly guy.

At the end of the night—early morning, technically—Harvey finally spoke to me. "Ready to go?"

"Can't wait." I threw my shawl around my shoulders, then slipped on my shoes, clutched my purse, and marched for the door. I imagined leaving a stream of frigid air in my wake as I strode to the car and let myself in. I tossed the keys onto the driver's seat.

Harvey climbed in and swiped them without comment. While I picked at the edge of my fingernail, he drove in silence for all of two minutes.

"Did you have a good time?" His tone was stiff.

"Yes. You?"

"Yep."

Liars, the both of us.

Two more minutes of silence.

I watched white road lines flash outside my window and felt Harvey's intermittent gaze on me.

"So what's wrong?" he finally asked. "I can tell something's bothering you, but that doesn't mean I can read your mind."

Apparently, all I'd needed was an opening, because once he provided it, I turned to him with no hesitation. "You pretended to be my friend just to get me to the wedding. Then you made fun of me because you were embarrassed to be seen with me."

"What? I did not." He looked at me like I was crazy.

Another strike against him. "If I didn't want to be seen with you, why would I have asked you to come?"

"For Sarah, of course. You're the one who just called me her 'gift.' Clearly that's all I am to you."

"That's not true." He seemed to struggle to keep his focus on the road. "Maybe I shouldn't have worded it like that to her, I admit. I wasn't even going to take credit for you being there." He rapped his knuckles against the steering wheel. "But I was ticked."

"Makes two of us. It was bad enough that I was just someone to provide butterflies and then transport your car." I replayed his words and laughter at the bar. "But to talk about me like that." My eyes closed briefly, the full hurt and anger crushing me. "The way you did with those guys . . . that was cruel and humiliating."

He shook his head. "I still don't know what you're talking about."

He was going to make me repeat it? I squeezed my purse. "I heard you say I was just a terrible pink-haired embarrassment that you couldn't wait to get rid of and forget about. You laughed at me. You led me on all this time, just so you could get me to the wedding for Sarah—which was nice for her, but also kind of messed up. I'm not a gift. I'm not an object. And I have feelings, no matter how weird you think I am."

"Hey, weird was Sally's word, not mine. But as for everything else, you're wrong. I didn't make fun of you."

"You said you only brought me there for Sarah, that after tonight, you couldn't wait to get rid of me. Don't deny it. I heard you at the bar. Every word." Or mostly, anyway. Enough. More than enough.

I stared out the windshield.

The low hum of the car motor was all I heard for the longest time. If I'd been secretly, desperately hoping for an emphatic denial or plea for forgiveness, I didn't get it.

Instead, Harvey's sudden loud guffaw made me flinch against my seat belt.

I gasped. "You think it's funny?"

Still laughing, he appeared to be trying to catch his breath as he nodded. "I do. Hilarious." He held up a hand and spread his fingers wide.

"No, listen. It's funny because you've got it all wrong. I wasn't talking about you, I was talking about that." He thrust a thumb over his shoulder. I turned my head to see what he was pointing at and spotted his discarded tie lying on the back seat.

The *salmon*-colored tie.

I swallowed, realization descending in an uncomfortable fog.

"Yep." He nodded. "That's the 'lame pink embarrassment' the guys and I were laughing about. The stupid ties Sally made us wear."

Heat crept up my neck.

"I'm sorry if you thought I was referring to you, but I guess that's what you get for eavesdropping."

"I wasn't eavesdropping. I was only trying to get a glass of water. And that wasn't all I heard." My voice came out strained. "You said every time I talk, you have to pretend to be interested."

His brow puckered, and I imagined him searching

his memory.

"You can't explain that one away." But I wanted him to. *Please.*

He laughed again. "I wasn't talking about you, I was talking about Sally, how every time she talked about the wedding, she'd go on and on with all these little details about sprinkled donuts and fancy paper fans and—man, it was so *boring.*"

His smile dropped and a muscle in his jaw flickered. "But you jumped to conclusions, and if you really believe I'm the kind of guy who would make fun of you behind your back—especially about something so superficial as the color of your hair—what can I say?"

He paused while he turned the wheel harder than necessary. "I guess it's really not funny after all."

Emotions clogged my throat and sadness smothered me. I fumbled with my purse, clasping and unclasping it, needing to pretend to do something. I felt sick. This drive was taking forever.

I had to apologize, but before I could manage the words, he continued. "Maybe we'd both be better off if you just go back to living in your—your safe little cocoon."

My ears buzzed. "Chrysalis."

"What?"

I tapped my nails against my purse. "If you're trying to be clever and sarcastic and metaphorical by referring to butterflies, the correct term is *chrysalis*. A butterfly forms inside of a chrysalis, not a cocoon. Cocoons are made by moths."

"Like it matters." His tone couldn't have been more

derisive. Silence followed, prickling my skin.

He raked a hand through his hair. "I enjoy your company, your friendship. I thought maybe we had a good thing starting, but you—" He muttered something under his breath.

My heart stuttered. Against my better judgment, I whispered, "What?"

He shot me a searing look. "You ditched me and started cozying up to that other guy."

"What? I didn't—"

"Even if you don't have experience dating, common sense should tell you it's not cool to blow off your date to dance with another guy."

There. There it was. He'd finally called me his date, but I couldn't rejoice.

It was too late.

"But I thought you didn't want to dance with me anymore. I saw you dancing with Amber."

"I was just waiting for you. And Amber? Please. I owed her one. We practically grew up together. She's like a sister to me, that's all. But I'm guessing that guy wasn't your brother."

My brother.

How could he? His words burned me. Outwardly, I didn't move. But inside, I recoiled as if he'd struck me.

I stared at my trembling hands. Sweat sparkled on my palms like glitter—ugliness masquerading as something beautiful.

The car swung around a bend and my stomach went with it.

My brother.

I *had* danced with him, long ago . . . when he was a sweet, chubby two-year-old and I was twelve. A lifetime ago.

He'd had an obnoxious, fat frog toy that played an inordinately happy, bouncy song.

I could hear it now. *"Froggy went a-courtin' and he did ride, uh-huh . . ."*

He'd loved that toy, that song.

"Froggy-woggy, *sing!*" he'd say, punching the toy's belly to start the music. Then I'd scoop Matt up and frolic around the room with him. His soft fuzzy hair tickled my nose, and he smelled like baby shampoo.

He shrieked with delight, giggling, his laughter throaty and irresistible.

But he quickly became too heavy for me to hold. When I had to plop him back down, he immediately lifted his pudgy arms, demanding, "A *den!* A *den!*" His way of saying "again."

"A *den*, Lie-Lie!"

Lie-Lie, his way of saying Lila.

What I wouldn't give to hear him call me that again, to hold him one more time, feel his heaviness in my arms instead of in my heart.

My arms fell weak at the memory.

Harvey said something, but I didn't hear it.

I didn't care.

I couldn't get enough oxygen. My desire to escape the crushing sorrow and the confined space of the car was so strong that when the tires ground to a halt at a stop sign, in a location I recognized, my voice came out raspy. "I-I'm sorry"—I grasped the door handle—"I just can't deal with this right now."

I swung my door open.

"Hey!" Harvey's face flashed alarm. "No, don't—" He reached for me as my hand fumbled for my purse, spilling my phone. I pulled away.

My phone dropped from the car to the road, and I fled for the shadows.

Chapter 18

I thought I heard Harvey yell my name, but my buzzing ears couldn't be trusted. I was fairly certain I heard a horn honk and tires screech.

Ready to double over with grief, I pressed myself against the darkness of a tree trunk, wishing I could meld with its solid sturdiness. Instead, I slid to a sitting position, wilting into the shadow, my sorrow consuming me.

Matt, my brother.

Gone.

Mags, gone.

My mother, my father, all gone.

Nothing and no one could replace them. No friendship. No relationship.

Tears rolled and dripped. Harvey's cold reference to my brother had been horrible. Unforgivable.

A car crept by. Was it him? Was Harvey looking for me? If so, I didn't care.

My family filled my mind, my heart, my soul.

I had room for nothing more.

Apart from my silent, shuddery sobs, I stayed still, hugging my skirt tight against my legs, turning invisible in this dark, sleeping world, yearning to vanish into the comfort of isolation.

My cocoon.

~

My legs fell asleep beneath me, but my mind refused to shut down and let me rest.

At last, I stood. Rigid and alert, I listened for an engine and watched for headlights. When I detected a vehicle approaching, I froze in the shadows. After long minutes of silence, I peeked out and verified the road was clear before weaving my way through neighborhood streets and following sidewalks.

I was surprised by the number of windows with no curtains drawn and TVs still flickering. Were the people asleep? Didn't they care that strangers could peer into their homes?

I found myself wondering about the families inside. Were they functional and happy, or messed up and miserable? A blend of something in between?

Did they know what loss was? And if so, how did they survive it?

I didn't want to be noticed by anyone. I wondered how invisible the shadows made me in my pale dress. Clouds obscured the stars, the night sky pressed down on me, but I counted the darkness as my ally.

Hot as the day had been, a cool breeze hit me, and I shivered.

I knew my way home from here, but the walk would be long. In the car, my desperation had skewed logic, and the distance hadn't seemed far. My feet were already sore, and these shoes weren't made for hiking. I slipped one off and tried to snap off the heel, but it wouldn't budge. Cheap shoes shouldn't be so well made.

I turned back and retraced my steps to where I'd jumped out of Harvey's car.

With any luck, I'd find my phone and call a ride.

At the edge of the intersection, I paused, easily spotting broken pieces of my phone. Great. So much for that.

I kicked off my shoes, left them where they fell, and began walking in stocking feet. My pantyhose were destined for the garbage. But at least my bare soles were tough.

Who'd have guessed my habit of walking barefoot would prepare me for this?

The residential street ran out into a stretch of overgrown lots bordered by metal fences. I crossed a railroad track and found myself missing the presence of the homes. A parking lot gave way to a strip of factories before the street curved around a bend. Part of the sidewalk had been dug up and taped off. Dirt and gravel lay scattered near a small pit.

I stepped through the grass, trying to avoid stones, and peered down the hill. About two miles to go. My calf muscles ached.

Before long, I gave up on the shadows and found myself gravitating to more illuminated spots. I looked up and down the streets, almost searching for Harvey's car, almost to the point where I wanted to see it, because thinking about who else might be out at this hour chilled me.

Would anyone hear me if I screamed? I walked along a barely lit vacant parking lot near an empty strip mall. My arms and legs prickled. Had I simply traded one bad situation for another?

A worse one?

My shoulder blades tightened and tingled as I caught the sound of an approaching engine.

Keep driving, keep driving, my mind chanted. Or did I pray it?

Good idea. God was the only one out here I could trust. *Lord, please keep me safe.*

The engine puttered on the road to my left, and I increased my pace, my back stiff, head high, desperately acting as if being out for a shoeless stroll at this hour was normal. My blisters smarted and my heels throbbed, but my shaky knees and pounding heart worried me the most.

Keep driving, keep driving.

The vehicle pulled closer and idled beside me, throwing a kink in my breathing.

"Lila?"

The man knew my name. And while the voice didn't belong to Harvey, it was familiar.

I turned. "Jay?" Relief flooded me, the intensity of it astounding me.

He frowned, his face a complex range of unreadable expressions. "What in the world are you doing out here?"

I glanced up at the sky, spotted one star. Or was it an airplane? "Nice night for a walk, don't you think?" I considered a shrug but didn't have the energy. What must he think of me, such a "nice" girl, wandering the streets at this hour?

He left his car with an angry slam of the door. A moment later, he put his hand on my arm and looked me in the eye. "What's going on? Are you okay?"

I nodded, suddenly overcome with a desire to cry. But I sucked it back in and stilled my face muscles. "Just tired."

"Come on, I'm taking you home." His arm slipped securely around me, and until that moment, I didn't realize the full extent of how unsafe I'd felt.

"How did this happen?" In the dome light of Jay's car, I noticed his jaw set tight as I buckled my seat belt.

I sighed, not up for explaining my situation but figuring I owed it to him.

How did this happen, indeed? A beautiful day had spiraled out of control and crashed into a million devastating pieces. "The guy I was with—he was driving me home and we got into a . . . disagreement."

"A fight? And he kicked you out? What a—"

"No, he didn't. I got out. It was my choice." I rubbed my temples. "Not a very smart one, I realize that now."

"He shouldn't have left you."

"I'm sure he didn't want to. He probably came back looking for me, but I—I don't think he could see me. I wasn't trying to be found."

"You were scared of him."

I caught the edge of my lip between my teeth. "No, I overreacted."

Jay's face darkened. "You trusted your gut. That's not overreacting."

I leaned back against the headrest. "I really appreciate your help, but please, can we go? I'd like to get home." And go to bed and sleep for a week.

"Of course." He shifted the car into drive, and I gave him directions.

I wanted my mind to stop questioning everything, but it continued churning. "I can't believe you found me." I turned to Jay. "Didn't you leave the reception a while ago?"

"Not that long ago. I live out of town, so I reserved a hotel. But there was some kind of mix-up. The place claimed they didn't have my reservation, and they were all booked up. So I figured I'd just head for home and stop somewhere if I got tired."

We turned onto a rural road and approached my street. *Almost there.* I fought a yawn.

Jay cleared his throat. "You won't be going out with that guy again, will you?"

I followed the arc of the headlights as they swept up my driveway. "Highly doubtful."

Jay slanted a disapproving look my way.

"I mean, no, I'm not planning on it." My words still sounded too open-ended. Plans could change.

"Any guy who'd treat you like that doesn't deserve a second chance." Jay parked the car with a slight jolt.

His words and tone unsettled me. I knew he meant well, but . . . "He's not a bad guy, really. And you don't know him, so—"

"I know enough. You were walking home alone in the dark at one in the morning. Enough said."

I unbuckled my seat belt and clasped my purse. "Thanks for the ride."

"You bet." He jumped out. "I'll walk you up."

At my door, as I drew out my key, he said, "I'm sorry you didn't have a better night, but you at least enjoyed some of it, right?" His fingers brushed my shoulder and his voice lowered. "The parts you spent with me, maybe?"

The hint of hope in his voice made me turn. The look in his eyes confused me, held me—as did his hand on my back. His face was near, and leaning nearer.

I set my hand against his chest and pressed gently as I stepped back. "I'm sorry, I . . ." Was I misreading this situation, or was he trying to kiss me? I turned and inserted my key, bending my head over it more than necessary. "I'm just really tired . . ."

"Of course. Sorry for keeping you. Please, go on." He motioned at the door, indicating I should go in.

My hand paused on the knob, which I'd already unlocked, and now I wondered if I should have. Was I jumping to wild conclusions again? I had a sudden feeling that if I opened the door, Jay might follow me in. He didn't seem in any hurry to leave.

He just wants to see me in safely, that's all.

His smile lingered, patient and pleasant. "Relax, I know you're not going to invite me in. I know you're not that kind of girl. I like that about you. But tell me, Lila, truthfully, without overthinking or second-guessing—did you enjoy your time with me tonight?"

I swallowed, the second-guessing beginning. I nodded, feeling vulnerable.

"Good, because I enjoyed my time with you. Very much. We seem pretty right for each other, don't you think?"

"We hardly know each other." I turned my doorknob slowly, blocking the action with my body while keeping my attention on Jay.

"Relax," he repeated, "I'm not trying to freak you out, but that's where you're heading—if you're not already there—isn't it? Just let me ask you something. Do you know what the *J* stands for?"

"What? What do you mean?" But I didn't really want to know. I opened my door just enough for me to dart inside. I swung it closed, but not all the way—his arm and shoulder stopped it.

"Whoa, called it." He smiled. "Seriously, please don't be afraid. I'm not a stranger. You know me."

I pushed my weight against the door, accomplishing nothing but increasing my heart rate. "A few dances and moments of conversation hardly count as knowing someone—"

"Obviously. That's the problem you had with the other guy. Hey, calm down. It's okay, really. Just hear me out. That's all I'm asking—just give me one second."

He held up his finger. "You know how I introduced myself as Jay? That isn't a name, it's a letter. It stands for my name."

As if I cared.

"Jess. My name's Jess, as in your computer-friend Jess."

He stuck his hand through the gap in my door, as if offering it to me to shake.

I blinked.

"I have to say," he went on, "it's sure nice to finally meet you in person."

Chapter 19

"Jess?" I gasped. Homeschool-forum Jess?

"The one and only." His amusement shone clear as he eyed me through the gap in the door.

The pathways to my brain closed. "But you're—you're a guy." At some point in my stunned state, my muscles weakened, and Jess pushed the door open and stepped inside.

Confusion replaced my fright. "Jess is a girl."

"Nope, definitely not." He took my arm and led me to my couch, where he sat down beside me.

"But you told me—"

"I didn't. That was just an assumption you made when we first started chatting."

That couldn't be right. I searched my memory. "You lied to me."

"I didn't. You jumped to conclusions. I just didn't correct your mistake."

"That's still a lie—a lie by omission."

"I didn't correct you because I liked talking to you.

You made it clear that you never chatted with guys. I didn't want you to block me."

Jess took my hand. "Look at me. I'm still just me, your friend."

I tried. I searched his face, his eyes, but I still felt like I was looking at a stranger.

"You can trust me. We've known each other for years. You know how long I've wanted to meet you. If I could have done this any other way, I would have. But I got tired of waiting, so when things finally lined up and I got this chance, I grabbed it."

His thumb traced my knuckles. "I know you don't like surprises, but I think it all worked out, so it's okay." He waited. "Say it's okay?"

I shook my head, blood roaring through my veins. I pulled my hand away. "It isn't. Do you have any idea how . . . *betrayed* I feel right now?"

He sighed and rubbed his dark hair, messing it. "I do. That's just it, I do. But this time, I'm here in person to talk you down. I'm not limited by typing on a keyboard. This is better."

"You're not hearing me. I can't—I can't suddenly be okay with the fact that you hid who you really are all this time."

"So I'll give you time." He frowned and put his palms on his knees, staring down at them. "But try to keep this in perspective. It's one small detail, that's all."

"It's a big detail. Monumental."

"One small detail," he repeated. "Everything else was true."

Really? What if he was just someone who lurked on

the site, one of those creeps my parents had warned me about? "Were you ever even really a homeschooler?"

"Of course I was."

My lips pinched briefly. "Did your parents really die, or did you make that up just to have something else in common with me?"

"No way, I'd never do something like that. I told you—everything else was true." He touched my hand again. "Just give it some time to sink in. Sleep on it. You're exhausted. It'll make more sense tomorrow. You won't be mad at me tomorrow."

I slid away into the corner of the couch, my mind still racing. "How did you find me?" I was always so careful. "How did you end up at the wedding? Did you really know the groom?" *Please say yes.*

"No, of course not. Don't hold that against me. Actually"—he spoke in a conspiratorial tone out of the corner of his mouth—"I was doing the guy a favor. Did you see the turnout on his side of the church? He needed all the help he could get."

I gave an exasperated sigh but was struck by how Jess-like that comment sounded.

He stretched his legs and rested his shiny black shoes on my coffee table. "Don't forget, you did invite me."

"What?" My mind scrambled, then realized what he meant. "I said after the wedding."

He spread his hands. "It's after the wedding. I was just a little early, that's all."

"How'd you find me?" I asked again.

"You sent me that picture of you and Harvey at the park."

The photo flashed through my mind, and I saw my mistake. "We were standing near the sign."

He nodded. "I zoomed in and read it. Did a search, and bingo—found the name of your town. From there, locating the time and location of a wedding, for a Sarah, on the date you told me, was easy. So easy you might have seen me coming if you weren't so distracted by that other guy."

He knew so much about me and Harvey, and the realization hit me like a fresh invasion of privacy. I was gripped by an urge to bury my head under a couch cushion. Only I hadn't vacuumed under them in months. Maybe even a year.

Then I realized I wasn't the one who should be ashamed. I aimed a hard gaze at Jess. "That's creepy and stalkerish. After you did all that, did you really think I'd be happy to see you?"

Jess plucked a fuzz off the leg of his black pants. "No, I knew we'd have to talk through some stuff first, which is why I didn't drop this on you at the wedding. Plus I wanted you to get a chance to enjoy my company without knowing who I was. So you'd see you really do like me. Even though I'm a guy." He turned his expressive eyes on me. "And I know you'll forgive me. You've got a heart of gold."

"Please." Disgust coated my voice. "I'm naive, you mean."

"No." His voice was firm, but kind. "Don't listen to people who call you that. They're really just jealous of your goodness and innocence. They don't appreciate the real you if they're trying to change you. I like you just the way you—"

I held up my hands. "Stop. Just stop. This is too much, and it's too late. I can't do this tonight. I need you to go, please."

"Lila, do you realize what I did for you today? I was here when you needed me, every time. Harvey treated you like dirt. One of the reasons I had to come find you was him. I've had a bad feeling about him from the start."

"Clearly. You do realize there's a name for that, don't you? Jealousy."

Jess's eye twitched. "Call it what you want. But if it weren't for me, you'd still be walking the street—*if* you were lucky and not snatched up by some creep."

I think maybe I was.

Lord, how do I get out of this?

Jess still hadn't made a move to leave, and my only phone lay smashed on the road.

Don't make him angry. Was my mind working overtime, or did it sense danger?

"You left the reception when we did, didn't you? You never went to a hotel—you followed us."

"Only because I was concerned for you, afraid Harvey would hurt you, and I was right. I saw him shove you out of his car, then take off like a coward. The only reason I didn't chase him down was there was no way I was going to leave you alone. I stayed out of sight till you were ready for me."

My brow scrunched. He'd been lurking in the shadows the whole time? And I'd thought I'd been so careful, so invisible.

"If you could just forget that other guy—"

"He didn't push me." I slapped my foot against the hardwood floor for emphasis.

"I know what I saw."

"You saw what you wanted to see."

"And you only believe what you want to believe." A thread of irritation slipped into his voice. "Holding out for some made up 'Mr. Right' when I'm sitting right here. We've got more than five years of interactions and relationship. Good times, hard times. You've only had days with him."

"Weeks," I clarified, "but that was different. It was all in person—not through a computer screen."

"Whose fault is that? I would've been here in person a long time ago if you would've let me." He leaned forward. "Let me now. That's all I'm asking for, a chance."

I studied him still perched on my couch as if he wasn't going anywhere. "I think it's time you found your hotel."

Jess sat back, stretched his arms out, and rested them behind his head. "You've got this entire house with a couch and a spare bedroom, I came all this way for you and the night's almost over, and you can't just let me crash here for a few hours?"

I stared at him.

He stood. "Fine, I knew you'd never go for that, but I had to give it a shot." He loosened his tie so that it hung crooked. "It's okay. At least you let me in your house, your secret refuge." He winked. "For you, that's huge progress. I'll take it."

I crossed my arms. "'Let' you is a stretch, don't you think? I seem to recall you forcing your way in."

The corners of his eyes crinkled. "Come on, you would've let me in eventually. I was just speeding things up."

I tried to lead Jess to the front door, but he strolled in the opposite direction. "I guess it's too late to ask for a full tour, but I'd really like to see your butterfly room."

He disappeared around a corner and snapped on the dining room light.

"Hey, the light will disturb them." I caught up to Jess as he stood gazing at the resting butterflies and rows of chrysalises hanging like milky green pendants.

He let out a low whistle. "Cool. Very cool. You really are incredible."

"No, what I am is tired." Overwhelmed. Did my tone sound as desperate as I felt? "Please, I need you to go."

"The room's just like I always pictured it."

"Please." I tugged at his arm. A mistake, I realized when his head whirled and his hand caught mine with a strength that surprised me, frightened me.

"Please," he echoed, his voice odd, his intense eyes and grip telling me he meant something entirely different than I had. "Lila . . ."

The yearning in his tone made me back away. I wasn't sure what I saw in his gaze—but I knew I didn't trust it.

Jess closed the small space between us, forcing me against the wall. His hands pinned my wrists like shackles. Panic closed around my heart.

His mouth came down on mine, hard, bruising my lips. Horrified, I fought for air and tried to wrench myself away, my soul screaming.

No first kiss should ever feel like this, like suffocating, like dying.

Fierce pounding filled my head, and Jess pulled away abruptly as if he heard it too.

And that's when I realized he did—because, thank God, someone was banging on my front door.

Chapter 20

The pounding increased, sparking hope in my anguished heart.

Lord, did You send help?

"I'll get it." Jess strode for the door.

I raced forward, ready to yell for help. "No, this is my house—"

"And no one should be disturbing you at this time of night."

"Oh? Only you?" I fought the trembling in my muscles.

Jess blocked me with his body as he opened the door.

Catching a whiff of peppermint, I stuck my head over Jess's elbow and saw Harvey standing on my front porch, looking stunned.

His silence unnerved me. So did the partial smile creeping across Jess's face. All at once, I realized Harvey was drawing horrible conclusions.

He looked at me, and hurt flashed in his eyes before a blank, cold shadow shuttered his gaze. With his ragged hair and wrinkled shirt, he appeared thoroughly disheveled and tired.

"Hey, man. What're you doing here?" From Jess's tone, he might as well have said, "Get lost."

"Harvey." My voice drew his gaze. "This isn't what it looks like."

"You got home okay." His voice sounded strained. "That's all I need to know."

"No, it's not. Listen to me—I'm sorry about everything—"

"Whoa, do *not* apologize to this guy." Jess adjusted his stance and nudged me back with his elbow before refocusing on Harvey. "I saw how you treated her. Get off this property before I call the cops."

"Shut up, Jess!" I stomped on his foot and broke past him, out into the night air.

At Harvey's side, relief filled me. I looked up at him, but he eyed me warily, like he didn't know me. It broke my heart.

I touched his arm. He tensed, almost moved away. I could barely hear his words, yet the pain behind them rang clear. "You never once let me into your house."

A train whistle howled mournfully in the distance, trying to distract me from what I had to say. "I didn't let him in, either. He gave me a ride home, and—" I couldn't even voice what he'd just done—"and now he won't leave."

"She doesn't want me to leave." Jess joined us on the porch and closed the door behind him. "Once you're out of the picture, she'll realize that."

I whirled on Jess. "What's the matter with you? Do

you hear yourself? You need to leave. Now."

Harvey's arm came around me as he faced Jess. "You better do what she says."

"Yeah? Or what? She's gonna sic the butterflies on me?" He snickered and strolled to the grass. "Or will she sic you? Frankly, I think the butterflies would do more damage."

"What's your problem?" Harvey stalked after him. "You looking for a fight?"

"I'm looking to pay you back for the way you've been treating her, so yeah." Jess faced Harvey and moved his arms in a warm-up motion. "Punching you might suffice."

Harvey braced his stance, biceps tensing, fists curling. "Bring it."

Harvey stood taller, his muscles more defined than Jess's, yet Jess sidled up to him with a confidence that scared me.

I ran forward. "Stop this, both of you! No one's fighting anyone." I stepped between them and faced Harvey. "Come on, this is stupid. If he won't go, we will. And then we'll call the police."

Every muscle in Harvey's face remained tense.

"Please."

Harvey looked torn, almost disappointed, like he really wanted to fight, but my plea must have meant something to him because he took my hand and turned for the house.

A moment later, Jess appeared in front of us. With no warning, he slammed his fist into Harvey's face.

Harvey bellowed and staggered back, unintentionally jerking me. My hand sprang open in alarm, letting him go.

Jess struck him again, and Harvey fell. Hard.

His face hit the ground and he groaned into the grass. Clutching at the earth, he struggled to get up.

Jess resumed a fighting stance.

"Stop!" I shrieked, finally finding my voice. I rushed Jess and shoved him. "Get away from him! He never even tried to hit you."

"Because I didn't give him the chance." Jess slipped his fingers through my hair and slid a strand behind my ear.

Shuddering, I batted his hands off me. I tried again to push him away, but he was much more solid than he looked.

"You're not being very nice, Lila. I fight for your honor, and this is how you repay me?"

"I don't owe you anything."

His lips mashed together and he seized my wrists. I suddenly wished I didn't live in such a secluded location. Trees cut off all visibility from the street. Neighbors didn't live within shouting distance. My safe haven had betrayed me.

From the ground, Harvey suddenly grabbed Jess's ankles, throwing him off balance. Instinctively, Jess released me, but he still fell.

Harvey landed a fist to Jess's face. The two rolled, fighting and grunting until Jess managed to jump back up, eyes flashing. He kicked Harvey in the ribs repeatedly, as if he'd never stop.

"I'm calling the police!" I raced for my house. Jess

wouldn't know it was a lie, that I didn't have a phone.

He caught me on the porch. At least I'd gotten him away from Harvey.

My mind scrambled. "Jess, you have to leave. Please, just leave."

He worked his jaw, his gaze intense. "I came all this way for you."

My gaze kept returning to Harvey. I had to help him. "Let me tell Harvey to leave. Then I'll go back inside with you. We can talk."

Jess laughed. "Tell him to go, sure. But we won't be going back inside."

I swallowed, deciding not to analyze that statement, and hurried to Harvey's side. He drew the back of his hand across his mouth and coughed.

I dropped to my knees, and he winced when I touched his shoulder. "Hey," I said softly.

He groaned, but something told me it was more from frustration than pain. Shadows blended with his cuts and bruises.

He touched my face. "You need to get out of here. Take these." He shoved something hard and cold into my hands. His phone and car keys.

I palmed them, my fingers pausing on his. "I really am sorry about earlier."

"So am I. I shouldn't have gotten jealous and lost my temper."

Jess appeared above us, his presence increasing the darkness.

Harvey spat and struggled to sit up, but Jess's foot to his chest shoved him back down.

I gasped in dismay as Jess yanked the phone and keys from my hand and chucked them far into the trees.

Harvey's gaze snagged on Jess's car. Something registered on his face. "You're the one who honked and forced me through that intersection." He looked at me. "I turned around and came back for you, but I couldn't find you."

I knew it. "It wasn't your fault."

"And then I found her and rescued her." Jess's voice intruded. "You had your chance, pal, and you blew it." Jess locked one arm through mine and tugged. "Let's go, Lila."

"I'm not going anywhere with you." I planted my heels, straining in Harvey's direction.

"Have it your way." Jess released me, surprising me, and I stumbled back to Harvey and took his hand.

But the ease with which Jess had let me go unsettled me. Like it was too good to be true. I watched him walk away, but he paused at Harvey's car.

He pulled out a pocketknife, flicked it open, and proceeded to slash each tire.

Muffling a gasp, I squeezed Harvey's hand and placed myself in front of him as Jess headed back toward us, the knife still open.

Jess shouldered me aside and pressed the blade to Harvey's throat. I screamed, wanting to hit Jess or yank his arm away, but I was too afraid of bumping the knife.

Jess's face remained rigid. "Changed your mind yet?"

His meaning was clear. To protect Harvey, I had to go with him. I swallowed and nodded, took one last look at Harvey, who lay tense and sweating, motionless under the touch of the blade. His eyes were on Jess now, not me.

"Yes," I said, hoping to make Jess move. "I'll go with you."

"No," Harvey rasped.

Raising the knife, but not closing it, Jess reclaimed my arm, and we walked.

I felt no relief. I'd traded one hopeless situation for another.

This is my fault. I'm the reason Jess is here. The reason Harvey's hurt.

We passed Harvey's car, and I caught a whiff of rubber.

A lump of ice settled in the pit of my stomach as we headed for Jess's car.

"Where are we going?" My voice sounded distant.

"You like surprises?"

The ice rose to my throat. "You know I don't." I looked back and saw Harvey push himself up and shake his head, as if to clear it.

Jess opened the driver's door and nudged me in so that I had to crawl over to the passenger seat, where I discreetly tried the door. Locked.

"Buckle up." He slammed his door, then started the engine. Where had the knife gone? Tucked back in Jess's pocket, I supposed. Ready and waiting for the next time he wanted to threaten someone. I tried not to let my mind go there.

Suddenly Harvey appeared at Jess's window. He rattled the handle, banged on the car, and roared like someone in a horror movie. "Let her go!"

Jess ignored him and pulled away.

I strained for a glimpse of Harvey as he ran stumbling after us. "He'll call the cops."

"Eventually."

"You're not worried?" Jess's lack of concern chilled me.

"He's got nothing, so they'll have nothing."

I turned to Jess as we left my familiar street behind. "This is kidnapping."

"No, we're just taking a little trip."

"Against my will."

"You'll change your mind."

My hands fisted. "I won't."

He smiled as if he knew something I didn't.

"Jess . . . don't do this. You're not a criminal."

"I know that." He chucked my chin playfully, then stepped on the gas.

I edged myself closer to the door. "You can't make me love you."

"You were already getting there."

I let the silence speak for me, but he probably misread it.

"Attraction's like a science." Jess glanced at me. "That's why you always hear people talk about chemistry. I was awesome in chemistry, by the way. Top of my class." He chuckled, then spoke out of the corner of his mouth. "Bottom, too, but I focus on positives."

Positives. Maybe I should try that.

This guy used to be my friend, so maybe that meant he wouldn't hurt me.

Only . . . he already had.

"Once I get you to the right place, with the right controlled environment, it'll only be a matter of time before you learn to love me back, and then it won't be kidnapping because you'll want to be with me. How's that for logic?"

"Warped logic." My legs shook, and I told myself it was from anger. "You're crazy."

"Watch it." His steely tone increased my anxiety. The car accelerated with an abrupt burst of speed.

I shut my mouth and looked out the window. *Lord, what do I do?* There had to be something.

I fidgeted in my seat as Jess pulled onto the freeway. "You don't by chance need to stop for gas anytime soon, do you?" I leaned over to read the gauge, but he immediately blocked my attempt with his arm.

"Don't cross the center of the car while I'm driving, got it? I can't trust you yet. And no, I won't need to stop for gas anytime soon. We're all tanked up."

I waited a few seconds. "I'm really hungry, though." I sucked in my stomach, then released it, trying to make it prove my case with a growl. No luck. "Maybe—"

"I've got a big stash of energy bars in the back seat. Help yourself."

I blew a sigh through the corner of my mouth and reached for the plastic bag. I pulled it to the front, onto my lap, and made a show of examining a wrapper.

"'Only three ingredients,'" I read, "'walnuts, dates, and kale.'" I dropped the bar back into the bag. "Yum."

Jess nodded. "That's real food. Clean food. You could live on those."

My throat constricted, hoping that wasn't a foreshadowing of things to come. A vision of a cold basement room stocked with kale bars came to mind. "I think I prefer fake food. Dirty food." I looked longingly in the side mirror. A vehicle followed us and another one passed us, oblivious to my plight. Again, I tried the door handle.

"Um . . . I actually really need to use the bathroom."

"Sure you do."

I glared at him. "I do. Think about it. My last chance was at the reception, hours ago."

"We'll stop in a little while." He switched on some smooth jazz music, similar to what my dad used to listen to, and I wished I could travel back through a time warp.

How had my life become so screwed up?

How had Jess's?

I studied his profile. "What about all the other people in your life? Family, friends. You can't just bring me home with you and expect—"

"You know my parents are dead. They were my only family."

"But you must have friends."

"Acquaintances. No one close. No one who gets me like you do."

Like me. My heart clenched. *Please don't compare me to you.* "But what about all the things you used to talk about, the exciting things you went out and did, the parties, the people . . ."

He snorted. "Most of that was from whatever show I was watching that week."

What? Seriously? No wonder it had been so entertaining, so . . . unbelievable.

"Modern shows, of course. I knew you only watched classics."

I found my voice. "So if you weren't really doing all that stuff, what did you do with your time?"

"What did you do with yours? I kept myself plenty busy with chatting online, computer work, gaming."

He sounded as if he expected me to say congratulations. All I could manage was, "That's your life?"

He shot me an angry look, his eyes snapping. "Don't pity me. I had everything I needed. Everything except you."

I tried to stop my head from spinning. "And now you think we're going to . . . what? Hide from the world together?"

"Not hide—reject. We're good at that. Experts. Who needs any of them?"

Suddenly, I couldn't get enough air. *Me. I do.* "God didn't design us to live in isolation. He . . . He put a need—a craving—in us for more—"

"Right, it's 'not good for man to be alone.' So I'm remedying that." He smirked. "I'll be your Adam, and you'll be my Eve."

I tried not to gag. Would he expect me to have hundreds of children to populate our "world" as well?

My mouth prickled with dryness. "No person can be everything to someone." *Not unless that person is God.*

Dear God . . . He'd illuminated more truth to me in the last few minutes than I'd come anywhere close to in the last five years.

I listened to the tires whir over the road, racking up miles. I noticed the faintest fringe of light dawning on the eastern horizon and realized morning was coming. For some reason, that gave me a trace of hope—the visual promise of light pushing away the darkness. Like good vanquishing evil.

All things work for good shimmered through my mind, a verse from my religion-class days. Days of safety and security and family. I missed those days . . . had they prepared me for dealing with this? Somehow? Some way?

I moistened my lips. "All that stuff you said about God and religion being so important . . . I don't get it. You couldn't believe that and do this."

"This?" Jess repeated. "You mean taking you somewhere safe where you'll be loved and cared for? Yeah, real evil of me. Be honest with yourself, Lila. After you lost your parents, all you ever really wanted was someone to look after you."

"I'm not a child, Jess." Though maybe I'd been acting like one . . . *I can change. Lord, help me.*

Jess muttered something under his breath that sounded suspiciously like a curse. He hit the gas, jarring me against the seat belt.

I glanced out the back window and saw a single headlight growing larger as it drew closer. A motorcycle tailed us, growling and gaining.

Could it be?

My heart filled with hope. *Harvey?*

As if reading my mind, Jess flashed me a glare. "He's been behind us too long. Time to lose him." Jess swung into an abrupt turn, sending half the kale bars flying from the bag on my lap.

My heart thudded. It had to be Harvey. Only, how? He'd driven his car, and Jess had slashed the tires.

Then I remembered the motorcycle he'd stashed on the side of my yard.

My heart leapt.

Thank God for motorcycles.

Chapter 21

"You're going to kill us." My hands squeezed a kale bar, smushing it.

Jess drove recklessly in his attempt to lose Harvey, and I feared for everyone's safety. Lives could be gone in an instant. All it took was an unexpected curve, loose gravel, a fall, a crash.

Jess scowled. "He's an annoying pest."

In another situation, the words might have made me smile, since they were almost an echo of my original assessment of Harvey.

Harvey . . .

My every encounter with him flashed through my mind, churning my adrenaline, fueling my hope.

We'll get through this, we will. And we'll be stronger for it.

"You'd think he'd know when to give up."

He doesn't. He won't. My heart swelled.

Jess took a corner with tires squealing, and a horn blared.

If he kept driving like this, maybe someone would call the cops. I glanced in my mirror, then twisted in my seat. I'd lost sight of Harvey but had confidence he would come bursting back into sight any second now.

Any second.

I held my breath.

Any minute.

I bit my lip till it hurt.

Come on, Harvey. I'm counting on you . . .

My stomach dropped and I clutched the edge of my seat.

Please come back. Please find us again.

"We lost him." Jess's gloating words cut me. He wiped a trace of sweat from his temple, then sat straighter before glancing my way. "Hand me one of those bars."

Heat rolled through my veins, and I snapped. I grabbed handfuls of bars and chucked them at Jess's face, whapping him rapid-fire. "Stop this car *now* and let me out!"

Despite my performance, he barely swerved. He snatched my wrist and pressed hard. "Knock it off, Lila. What do you think you're accomplishing?"

My pulse pounded against his thumb.

Jess released me and turned the radio knob, cranking up the jazz, and I was disgusted at how right he was. My tantrum had accomplished nothing.

I brooded in my seat, turning my face to the window and rubbing my sore wrist. The sky had lightened enough that I could see more of our surroundings.

The world was waking up. The world that I'd

hidden from for so long.

Could it help me?

More traffic appeared.

A few minutes later, a red light forced Jess to stop.

Still facing the window, I straightened with an idea as a car slid to a halt beside us. A young woman, her hair cut in a short, sleek bob, sat sipping coffee, but her eyes stared straight ahead. I willed her to glance my way.

Nothing.

Lord, please.

She turned, and I silently mouthed, "Help."

I watched her expectantly, but she merely looked mildly confused.

Battling panic, I snuck my arm up and placed my hand near my ear, under cover of my hair, as if holding a phone. I mouthed, "Call help."

She frowned, then glanced away, and I sensed she didn't get it. I was only making her uncomfortable. Maybe she thought I was crazy.

But I couldn't settle for that, because if I didn't figure out something soon, I feared I'd have plenty of time to regret it. I'd go crazy for real—in isolation with Jess.

My life would be over before I'd even started living it.

Choosing to avoid people was one thing; being forced to avoid them was another thing entirely.

I wouldn't surrender without a fight. If I couldn't use muscle, I'd use brains.

I raised my hands to the window and lifted nine fingers, the way a child would show their age. I quickly followed with one finger.

Just as I was about to flash the final number, Jess hit the gas. He whapped my shoulder so hard, I smacked into the window.

Holding in a cry, I strained against my seat belt, trying to see the woman, but we'd already lost her car. I wasn't sure if she'd caught on to my signal or not, but I prayed she had and was calling the police with a description of Jess's car and, hopefully, the license plate number—though maybe that was expecting too much.

Jess changed lanes and made a sequence of fast turns, breathing heavily. "Don't pull crap like that, Lila." He spoke through clenched teeth. "I know you, and I know your weaknesses."

Refusing to let him scare me, I countered silently, *What are your weaknesses?* I racked my brain to recall something, anything useful from all our chats. Jess was cool, popular, fun, smart—or so I'd thought.

I was coming up with nothing useful.

"The next time you pull something stupid, a butterfly's gonna die. How'd you like that?"

I narrowed my eyes.

"I'll kill one, and I'll make you watch." He paused. "No, I'll make you do it. First, you'll have to pull off each wing, till you're left with just the pitiful little wriggling body, then—"

"Shut up, Jess." I scrunched the empty plastic bag in my hand. "You're cruel and disgusting and you're not going to make me do anything."

"We'll see about that." His jaw tensed and he adjusted his grip on the wheel. "We both know you're not really as brave as you're pretending to be. We both know you're cowering inside."

I was trying not to, but when I started thinking about what he might do next, my entire body tingled with fear.

I made myself take deep breaths and willed my heart rate to slow. I needed my mind to work clearly, to break this situation down and figure out one thing at a time.

First, I had to unlock the car so I could escape. Preferably at a stop, not with the road whizzing by.

Unlocking the car would require I reach the master button on Jess's side. That meant I'd need to distract him in a way that made his hands too busy to grab for me.

I recalled Jess's childish threat, complete with the unwanted image of a wingless butterfly. In my mind, I heard Harvey comparing butterflies to spiders, triggering my memory of Jess's weakness—*if* Jess had been telling the truth about it. Guess I'd soon find out.

In more rural countryside now, we approached a stop sign.

My chance.

I rested one hand near my seat belt latch, tense and ready.

The moment the car stopped, I turned to Jess but looked past him, at his headrest, making my eyes wide. "Wow, that's the biggest spider I've ever seen."

He almost turned, but didn't. "You're full of it."

"Full of what? *Bologna?*" I sniffed. "Think what you want."

Jess's cheek twitched. His foot remained on the brake as he obviously fought the urge to look.

I stretched my neck as if observing an arachnid creeping toward his neck.

Finally, he turned around, giving me the two seconds I needed.

I clicked myself free of the seat belt, then whipped the plastic bag over his head.

"Hey!"

In the moment it took Jess to yank the bag off, I'd hit the master lock on his side. Thrilled and terrified, I dove for my door.

He lunged for me as I burst from the car, but all he caught was a few strands of my hair.

I stumbled to the ground, scraped my knee, bounced back up, and skidded down an embankment. The thick skin of my feet resisted the pain. My ribcage pushed against my lungs, squeezing air from them.

Weaving past trees and through shrubbery, I ran, sure Jess was only a breath away, but I didn't dare pause to look. If ever I needed to fly, that time was now.

Racing through the dim dawn light, I pursued freedom, determined not to be recaptured. Not by fear, not by lies, and not by stupidity.

Air whooshed past my ears, and I thought I heard sirens somewhere in the distance. But I headed away, as if by instinct, from the vast visibility of the road. I ran till I had no breath left. And, like a creature drawn to nature, to hiding—because I still didn't know where Jess was—I ducked into an overgrown field, and the fragrance of wildflowers hit me like a heavenly perfume.

Sinking into the long, shielding grasses, I felt a measure of safety, despite the intense beating of my heart. I lay on my back and caught my breath, my adrenaline-spiked muscles and mind barely allowing it. But relief didn't come.

Fear, not for myself, but for Harvey, rippled through me, and I sat up, struck by panic. What had happened to him? Where was he now? Wounded as he was, he never should have climbed onto that motorcycle, let alone taken part in a high-speed chase. But he had.

He'd done it for me.

Then I remembered something else. He hadn't been wearing a helmet. I gripped my head in alarm.

The thought of him taking all those same sharp turns Jess had, especially without a helmet, terrified me. What if Harvey had wiped out and that's why we'd lost him?

The more I thought it, the more convinced I became.

What if he was lying back there in the gravel on some sideroad, bleeding to death? I almost fell to my knees.

Lord, no.

I burst up out of the grass, ignoring my protesting muscles, and waded back to the edge of the road. I couldn't sit and wait for help. Not if Harvey needed me.

He had come looking for me—now it was my turn to find him.

Gravel pressed into my feet, and I barely noticed. I ran toward a cluster of lights about a mile away. One of the lights burst out of the rest. It grew bigger, brighter, and seemed to be flying my way.

I rubbed my eyes, blinked, and saw the dazzling eye of one headlight. A motorcycle headlight.

The distinct roar of the engine jolted my heart rate. It couldn't be . . .

But I waited, almost mesmerized, by the side of the road, because I had hope, I had faith, and I had confidence. It had to be him.

Harvey.

I recognized his form and his face, bruised as it was, and his hair stood wild from the ride.

My eyes strangely damp, I ran forward as he ground the bike to a halt, leapt off, and raced to my side.

His gaze darted over me. "Are you okay?"

My heart panged. From the looks of him, he was the one who needed a doctor. I nodded, and he swept me into his arms and crushed me into a hug so tight I could barely breathe, and it was like I didn't even need to.

"You're safe now," he said, over and over. "The cops came."

I shivered, and Harvey held me tighter. In all my adult memory, I'd never felt a hug like this, so engulfing, so complete, so full of everything right and good that it could only be love.

And I hugged him back, hoping the motion conveyed what my words couldn't.

Inside me, wonder and joy danced with relief, kicking up bubbles, and I laughed into Harvey's shoulder.

He drew back. "What in the world could be funny right now?"

"You found me." I half choked on another laugh. "I can't believe you found me."

"That? That's nothing. I've always been good at finding you." He shook his head before pulling me close again. "Keeping up with me—that's been the real challenge. And after last night, I'd understand if you wanted to run away from me." He gave a short, wry laugh. "I seem to recall I promised you a great time."

I nodded. "And I'm still holding you to that. I'm not going anywhere." *Not without you.*

"Yeah?" Harvey spoke into my hair. "So you're not going to disappear back into your cocoon and hide from me?"

I glanced up at him with a smile. "My chrysalis, you mean? Nope, impossible. I broke free of it, and once you do that, you can't ever go back."

"Really?" His tone bounced with hope.

"Yep, that's just the way it works. That's the way God designed it." My heart expanded and fluttered, as if growing wings.

"So what now?"

"Now . . ." I gazed up and down the road, past the expanse of grass and trees and sky. "Now it's time to be free. Time to live."

Harvey's gaze followed mine, then returned to meet my eyes, almost hesitant. "Mind if I tag along?"

"I'd rather have you by my side."

"I like the sound of that." He stroked my hair tenderly, then nudged my toe. "But first, we really should do something about getting you a pair of shoes."

Epilogue

My doorbell rang, and instead of filling me with apprehension, the sound sent my spirits soaring.

I could get used to this.

I swiped pink gloss over my lips and dropped the tube into my purse before opening the door.

As expected, Harvey stood on my stoop.

As *not* expected, his hair shone blue. The unnatural, glaring color made my mouth drop open.

He gave a roguish grin. "Like it?"

I lifted a hand to shield my rising laughter. "It's very . . . blue."

"Right?" He turned his head to give me the full view.

My giggle escaped. "Looks like a bunch of blue morphos exploded on your head."

"Blue . . . whats?" He scratched his hairline. "I don't think that's what I was going for."

"Morphos. Big, gorgeous butterflies from the tropical region of—"

"Wait." He squinted one eye. "So you just called me

gorgeous?"

"No, I—I—"

"I think you did." He smiled smugly.

I floundered and redirected the conversation. "The color's great. In fact"—I struck a dramatic pose—"it's to 'dye' for."

"Oooh . . ." He gripped his chest as if I'd stabbed him. "Death by corny pun. Guess that's what I get for dating someone who talks to butterflies."

"I don't—" I paused and reminded myself I had nothing to hide. "I don't *usually* talk to butterflies."

"But when you do, they obviously don't tell you how much your jokes stink." He winked. "So just to be clear, you can make fun of my hair color, but your pink hair's off limits. I see the double standard."

His playful tone belied his words. "I figured I'd draw some of the attention off you and onto me, the way you prefer it, right?"

"My color's not that bad anymore." I touched a strand of my hair. "The pink's fading."

He stepped closer and looped his arm around my back. "Lila, it was never bad. And I only did this"—he pointed to his head—"to make you smile." He tapped my chin. "You have a great smile."

Maybe, but I preferred his. Thankfully, he'd healed well over these past two weeks. I was doing some healing too, most of mine on the inside. Seeing a therapist was helping, as was my newfound relationship with God.

"And," Harvey added, "now we can both look like a couple of rebellious bikers." He thrust out his chest.

"Though we may need to add a few tattoos for the full effect." He ran a palm over his neck. "Here, maybe? I was thinking of getting a big butterfly."

"Very funny." I reached up to touch his spiky hair, missing the blond. "It'll wash out, right?"

His eyebrows quirked. "That's for me to know and for you to wonder." He stepped off the porch. "I'll see if you're really with me for me, or just for my stunning good looks." He paused. "So don't be surprised if I shave my head bald next."

I rolled my eyes. "Do what you want. You won't get rid of me that easily." We stopped in front of his motorcycle and I eyed the two waiting helmets. "Asking me to ride this thing, though . . . That might do it."

"Come on, Lila, you promised you wouldn't chicken out." Harvey patted the seat. "You're gonna love it, you'll see."

"Hold on." I raised a finger and ran back to grab a flat rectangular present from inside my foyer. I held it out to him. "For Sarah. Can you put this in the saddlebag? But if it's too big, I guess we could always take my car."

"Nice try, but I'll make it fit."

Figured.

My gift sure didn't compare to his, this motorcycle, but I imagined Sarah would still appreciate it.

"Ready? Shoes on?"

I wrinkled my nose, then stuck out my foot, displaying the chunky boots he'd insisted I buy.

"Perfect." He held up a white helmet with a gaudy,

sparkly butterfly sticker centered on the front. "This thing's calling your name."

My lips twitched. "Classy touch, Harvey. Not cheesy at all." Intrigued despite myself, I peered closer. "It's not scratch-and-sniff by any chance, is it?" I loved those. Unable to resist, I scratched the wings, and a few sparkles gathered beneath my fingernail. After I gave the sticker a quick sniff, my lips dipped downward.

"Sorry to disappoint you, but now I guess I know what to get you for your birthday."

I envisioned sheets of colorful stickers, and the thought amused me.

With a bracing breath, I accepted the helmet and pulled it on. Harvey buckled it, then followed with his own helmet.

"Let's do this." He helped me on, and I felt as if I were settling onto the saddle of a metal beast. I assessed my situation and rubbed my sweaty palms. "I can't believe there aren't any seat belts on this thing."

"Just hold on to me really tight."

"And no roof," I muttered.

"That's called a car, Lila." He patted my knee and I almost fell off. Knowing he couldn't see my face clearly, I blushed freely.

"Hug the seat with your legs. I'll lean to turn, so just stay with me. And if you need me to stop for any reason, just tap me twice. Oh, and one more thing—it's gonna be loud."

No kidding.

He started the motor, and I couldn't believe I used to think his motorcycle was noisy from a distance—this thunderous volume put that sound to shame. The roaring vibrations coursed through me, doing their best to shake my ribs and arms loose. I tightened my grip. Nothing was going to make me let go of Harvey.

With a jolt, we took off on my first-ever motorcycle ride.

I'd almost been forced into my first ride two weeks ago when Harvey found me after I'd escaped from Jess. But the police had shown up in time, thanks to a certain lady in a car who'd understood my 911 plea.

The police had given us a ride to the hospital before questioning us in detail about everything that had happened.

Jess had tried his best to escape, but the cops caught him after a high-speed chase. With the multiple charges stacked against him, he wouldn't be getting out of jail anytime soon. Kind of ironic that he was going to end up being "institutionalized" after all.

I'd mourned for the loss of the friend I thought I'd had, but when I needed someone to talk to, I called Harvey or Sarah.

I imagined Jess would fill his plentiful hours attempting to write to pen pals. I shuddered, glad I wouldn't be one of them.

Now I gripped Harvey tighter, my fingers pressing into leather and solid muscle. The big world rushed by, and yet my entire world was right here, me and Harvey together. God was with us as well, His hand evident everywhere. We couldn't escape or ignore Him, and I no longer wanted to.

My pounding heart regulated itself as the miles flew

by. *I can do this.*
I am.

Sarah, who'd recently returned from her Caribbean honeymoon, shot out of her house the second we roared into the driveway.

"You got her on that thing? I can't believe it!" Sarah jumped up and down, hugged Harvey, whose hair didn't faze her, then moved on to me, her smile a pristine white in her tan face.

"Roger's got the grill going in the back. I'm so glad you could both come. I've got a five-pound photo album of honeymoon pictures I can't wait to show you."

"In that case"—Harvey grabbed his helmet—"we actually can't stay— Ouch!"

Sarah, of course, had whapped his arm. The sibling banter pricked my heart, reminding me of what I could have had with my brother and sister, but it also reminded me of what we did have. Those memories were mine to cherish forever.

"No way! For real?" Sarah's ecstatic reaction made me realize Harvey had just told her the bike was hers, and I felt fortunate to be a part of this happy moment in the here and now.

"It's no crystal vase, but—"

"Shut up! I thought you'd sold it!"

"That's what I wanted you to think."

"You tricked me." Sarah wagged her finger at him but didn't sound the least bit angry. "This is the coolest wedding present ever. If this is what you give, I may have to get married again. Build a whole collection."

She swiped a helmet and cruised out of the driveway. She raced up and down the street before returning and screeching to a stop.

When she climbed off, it was grudgingly. "I think we need to cancel this little dinner party so I can ride this thing all night. Wait'll Roger hears. We're gonna be fighting over this."

"Fighting?" Harvey shook his head. "So maybe not the best wedding gift after all?"

Sarah laughed. "We love making up—"

"Stop!" Harvey thrust his hands out and grimaced. "Quick, Lila, give her your gift."

I smirked, having a feeling he might regret his request, but handed my present over anyway.

"You two, you didn't have to get me anything. We just wanted to hang out with you . . ." Sarah pulled off the last piece of wrapping, studied the framed picture, then threw her head back and laughed.

Harvey peered over her shoulder and frowned down at the picture. Realization dawned as he saw the photo of himself chasing butterflies in my backyard.

He gaped at me. "What? You took a picture of that?"

"You know that's all I wanted to do that day—take pictures of butterflies. I guess you just happened to photobomb that one."

He groaned.

"I call it 'Chasing Your Dreams.'" After all, that was the day he'd started me realizing I didn't have to stay hidden away from the world.

"Oh, this is priceless." Sarah clutched her side. "This

is going up in the entryway, where everyone will see it."

"Awesome." Harvey narrowed his eyes at me.

I smiled and shrugged. "Someone once told me it's healthy to laugh at yourself."

He shook his head. "That kind of healthy makes me sick."

"Not too sick for some big steaks, I hope," Sarah said.

"Nope," I replied. *I'll eat anything but kale bars.*

"Come on, before Roger inhales them all." She led us into the backyard, where we greeted her husband and enjoyed the meal together, with lots of laughter. I felt part of a family again for the first time in years.

The food was great, but the company was better. I'd lost Jess, warped as that friendship had been, but I'd learned how to make new friends. Real ones.

After the meal, Sarah led me over to a small garden. "I'd really like to expand this and make it into more of a butterfly garden back here. Maybe you could help me."

"I'd love to. And if you want any milkweed plants, I've got plenty. You'll definitely attract monarchs if you add some of those."

Harvey looked up from his sports-related conversation with Roger. "Watch it, Sally. She'll turn your whole backyard into a weed patch. You'll get lost in it, and Roger won't find you for days." Harvey paused, then nudged Roger. "So on second thought, you might want to go for it."

"Funny, Harvey." Sarah tapped her chin. "You

speaking from experience? Do you get lost in gardens a lot? Or just at Lila's house?"

She pointed at her husband. "Roger's completely on board with my garden idea."

He gave a thumbs up. "Less yard to mow. Sounds good."

The guys resumed their conversation, and Sarah beamed at me with a knowing look.

"What?" I rubbed my lips self-consciously. "Is my mouth dirty?" Did I have steak sauce on my lips or something?

"No, I'm just so happy you guys finally found each other. And, just so you know"—she flipped her hair over her shoulder—"right before I messed things up between us—which I'm still totally sorry about, by the way—I was trying to convince Harvey to meet you." She dropped her voice. "But he wasn't interested. He thought you sounded like a dork."

I crossed my arms. "Yeah?"

"Don't tell him I said that." She glanced at him, then back to me. "Actually, I totally don't care." She smiled and added, "I kinda hope you do." She hugged me with one of her signature lung-crushing squeezes.

Like sister like brother.

"In fact"—she nudged me—"I'm gonna make a prediction. You two are totally gonna get married."

"Hey, Sarah," Roger called, saving me the awkwardness of having to come up with a reply. "Wanna show me that motorcycle now?"

"Finally!" She moved away but aimed her finger at me. "Remember, I totally called it!"

I shook my head as I watched her pull Roger around the side of the house and disappear from view.

"Called what?" Harvey joined me by the little garden and stood close enough to touch.

Cautious excitement zinged through me, anticipating that touch. "You tell me. She's your sister."

"Which means I couldn't tell you. She's wacky."

I sniffed a laugh. *Aren't we all?*

Sure made life fun.

"So you haven't said how you liked the motorcycle ride. Did you love it?"

"I did, actually." Just the thought sent my pulse racing. "It was like flying."

"So you'd do it again?"

"With you? Yes." I put my hands on my hips. "Even though you told Sarah you thought I was a dork."

"What? She told you that?" He glared in the direction she'd gone. "I'm taking that motorcycle back."

He regarded me seriously. "But hey, you know that can't count. That was before I met you and"—he smirked—"discovered just how much more of a dork you really are." He dodged a step away from me, as if expecting me to whack him. Sarah had conditioned him well.

"Oh yeah?" I eyed something near the house and edged toward it.

He nodded. "An adorable dork who elevates the word to the best kind of compliment."

"Great." With a stealthy hand, I secretly turned a small handle behind me. "If that's how it works, I want you to take this as a compliment, too." I grabbed the garden hose and aimed it at Harvey's hair.

Harvey sputtered as water hit him and blue dye ran down his face.

I laughed so hard, my full stomach began to ache.

He lifted his arms, now also streaked in blue. "I surrender!"

With a nod, I shut off the hose, then saw a flash of orange as two monarchs flew by. "Look!" I pointed. "Want to chase them? I could take another picture of you."

He let out something like a growl. "You'd better run, because the only thing I'm chasing is you."

I yelped, dropped the hose, and took off across the yard, dodging trees and bushes.

Risking a glance back, I turned and didn't see Harvey anywhere.

"Gotcha!"

I squealed as he pulled me into his strong arms and held me against his wet blue-streaked shirt.

I sighed contentedly, then breathed in the scent of garden hose, sun, and Harvey's skin. I snuggled against him, and my eyelashes fluttered against his bare bicep.

He looked down at his arm, then at me. "You know those are called butterfly kisses, right?" Hastily, he added, "I only know that from Sally."

Warmth spread up my neck and through my cheeks.

His voice lowered and turned husky. "I know you're all about butterflies, but when it comes to kisses"—he leaned down so that our faces almost touched—"I prefer the real thing."

His gaze held mine, searching, hoping.

"So do I." *At least, I think I do . . .*

I closed my eyes and leaned in till our lips fit together—warm, soft, and right.

Yes, I definitely do.

A Note from the Author

Thank you for spending time on my story, and I truly hope you enjoyed reading this novel as much as I did writing it. Maybe you'll even consider leaving a short review on Amazon?

Honestly, releasing a book can feel like dropping a labor of love into a black hole, so receiving a review—even just a sentence or two—can really make a writer's day!

And when you're looking for your next read, I hope you'll consider checking out my other books:

Past Suspicion
After losing her mother, Robin encounters mystery, tragedy, and romance in a small town full of big secrets.

Frozen Footprints
A missing twin. A desperate search. An isolated winter cabin. Where is Charlene's hero when she needs one most?

After the Thaw
Charlene's wounded heart must choose between her fiancé and the man whose past is more scarred than her own. But in choosing, she may just lose everything.

Acknowledgments

I'd like to thank my oldest daughter for sparking the inspiration for this story by asking me questions about butterflies one day last summer. The best ideas come in the most unexpected ways!

Thank you to my husband for supporting my desperate (yes, *desperate*) need to schedule some writing time into each busy week. If not for that, this novel would likely have been another year in the making.

As always, this story wouldn't be nearly as enjoyable if not for the feedback from my number-one quality-control readers, who just happen to be my sisters—who never let that stop them from being completely honest. (In the kindest way, of course. They provide dinner and cheesecake and candy while doing so!) Thanks, Monica and Cassandra, for never failing to point out the problems (both big and small) in my writing. I love that I can always count on you.

Sincere thanks to both my wonderful mom and my awesome brother-in-law Chris for making time to read this book when I needed new eyes on it.

Finally, thank You, dear Lord, for planting stories in my mind . . . I couldn't imagine life without writing. Thank You for this adventurous journey, and I look forward to the next chapter!

About the Author

Therese Heckenkamp was born in Australia but grew up in the United States as a homeschooled student. *The Butterfly Recluse* is her fourth novel and, in many ways, the story she was meant to write ever since she was five years old, considering that's when she wrote *My Pet Butterfly,* her very first "book."

Therese lives in Wisconsin with her husband, four energetic children, and, on occasion, a butterfly or two. As a busy stay-at-home mom and freelance proofreader, she fits in writing time whenever she can manage (and sometimes when she can't). She dreams up new stories mostly at night when the house is finally quiet.

Her previous novels have reached #1 bestseller in various Amazon Kindle categories, including Religious Romance, Religious Mysteries, and Inspirational Religious Fiction.

Therese looks forward to writing many more novels in the future. Visit her online to share feedback and to keep up-to-date on free ebooks, new releases, and more:

Therese's website: www.thereseheckenkamp.com

Goodreads: www.goodreads.com/ThereseH

Facebook: www.facebook.com/therese.heckenkamp

Twitter: www.twitter.com/THeckenkamp

Made in the USA
Monee, IL
03 May 2021